"I'M TIRED, LYN," HE CONFESSED. "I DON'T want to argue anymore. I don't want to think. Can't we call a truce, just for tonight?"

She felt the strength in him, the power that set him apart from other men, but she also sensed his vulnerability, and the risk he'd taken in showing it to her. Only a strong man would do that. Only a confident man. Only an innocent man . . .

"You know, if you give yourself up, they might not—"

"Didn't you hear anything I said?" he cried as he strode toward her.

He stopped in front of her and bent down, gripping the arms of the chair. His nearness unnerved her. His passion energized her. Her entire body kicked into high gear when he was near, and right now he was a whole lot nearer than she wanted him to be. "Please," she said without really knowing what she was asking. "Please, I—"

"I want your cooperation," he said, leaning so close she could feel the heat of his breath. "And I'm not real choosy about how I get it."

WHAT ARE *LOVESWEPT* ROMANCES?

They are stories of true romance and touching emotion. We believe those two very important ingredients are constants in our highly sensual and very believable stories in the LOVESWEPT line. Our goal is to give you, the reader, stories of consistently high quality that may sometimes make you laugh, sometimes make you cry, but are always fresh and creative and contain many delightful surprises within their pages.

Most romance fans read an enormous number of books. Those they truly love, they keep. Others may be traded with friends and soon forgotten. We hope that each LOVE-SWEPT romance will be a treasure—a "keeper." We will always try to publish

LOVE STORIES YOU'LL NEVER FORGET
BY AUTHORS YOU'LL ALWAYS REMEMBER

The Editors

BODY HEAT

RUTH
OWEN

BANTAM BOOKS
NEW YORK · TORONTO · LONDON · SYDNEY · AUCKLAND

BODY HEAT

A Bantam Book / November 1995

*If you would be interested in receiving protective vinyl covers for your
Loveswept books, please write to this address for information:*

Loveswept
Bantam Books
P.O. Box 985
Hicksville, NY 11802

ISBN 0-553-44429-8

Published simultaneously in the United States and Canada

PRINTED IN THE UNITED STATES OF AMERICA

OPM   0 9 8 7 6 5 4 3 2 1

To Carol Quinto, my critique partner,
for keeping this book and me on track,

And to my editor, Shauna Summers,
for not holding my feet too closely to
the fire.

PROLOGUE

"We'll be arriving at the Dallas–Fort Worth airport in twenty minutes, Mr. Brennermen."

Curt glanced from his notebook computer at the pretty flight attendant, noting the none-too-subtle invitation in her eyes. Sorry, darlin', he thought. This trip is strictly business. "Thanks for the warning," he drawled, giving her a smile that could break a woman's heart at fifty paces. "I've got a lot of work to do before we land."

Disappointed, the attendant headed back toward the galley of the first-class compartment. Curt resumed his work, but was interrupted again by the sharp jab of an elbow in his side.

"What'sa matter with you? She's *built*."

"Not interested, Benny," Curt answered, without looking up.

"Figures," grumbled his companion.

Curt gave a sidelong glance at the man beside him. Benny Fortuna was a massive man with a face that could stop a clock, but he had a heart as soft as butter. They'd met over five years ago, in a barroom brawl in the toughest, seediest, most dangerous dive in the jungles of South America. Curt had been jumped by several hired thugs, paid by a competitor who wanted to put an end to Brennermen's nearby oil-drilling operation. Benny had stepped in to even up the odds.

Curt had hired him on the spot as his bodyguard, a position he still held, though the fortunes of both men had drastically changed. Curt trusted the man with his life. But not, necessarily, with his private thoughts.

"This is a business trip, Benny. We've got a busy Thursday ahead of us. After we land I'm meeting with Halliburton about the pressure drilling equipment for the Siberian fields. Then it's lunch with Parker at Exxon, drinks with the state energy chairwoman, and finally the product launch at that security company we just bought."

"The Guardian gala," Benny said morosely. "Do we really have to show up at that? I know this great bar. . . ."

Curt's stern mouth pulled into a reluctant smile. Benny knew the "great bars" in every major city in the world. It was one of the many reasons that made him invaluable to a boss who'd spent most of the last two years of his life living out of a suitcase. "Business first."

"Yeah, but not business only," the big man argued. "Face it, boss. You've been pushing yourself for months without a break. It's not natural. A man's gotta have a little R and R, if you know what I mean."

Jewish mothers and chicken soup. Benny and sex. Both thought they were a magic cure for everything. There was a time when Curt might have agreed with him, but lately the thought of transitory relations had lost its attraction. Too often he'd woken up and looked into his partner's face, hoping against all reason to see a pair of cornflower-blue eyes.

Never look back.

Curt ran his fingers through the shaggy, light-colored hair he refused to cut to corporate standards, even though he owned one of the fastest-growing oil conglomerates in the world. In twenty-eight years he'd gone from riches to rags and back to riches again. Business magazines trumpeted his financial wizardry, but Curt knew his success was due to pure dumb luck. He'd spent five years rotting in a practically worthless wildcat oil operation, working his tail off to pay back a debt that was not of his making. If the wells hadn't come in two years ago, he'd still be there, along with the flies, filth, poverty, and political corruption.

The rocky ride had left scars on his body and soul, but he had only one regret. She's probably married by now, with a couple of kids . . . he thought.

"Boss? Are you okay?"

Benny's concerned tone brought him back to the present. Damn, it wasn't like him to drift off like that. Maybe he did need a little of Benny's R&R. "Tell you what. We'll make an appearance at the Guardian party, then slip out and do the town."

Benny's face lit up. "Now you're talking. I know this great place on the south side called the Blue Note, where . . ."

Curt smiled at his bodyguard's enthusiasm, but he didn't share it. One bar was as good as another—even the cities he'd seen in his international travels had begun to look the same. He had power, respect, and more wealth than he could spend in a dozen lifetimes. But that success hadn't come without a price. He'd had to sacrifice a few things along the way. Like his dreams. Like his belief in honesty, truth and justice, and all the other fairy tales he'd grown up with. Like the trust of an all-too-trusting girl with cornflower-blue eyes.

Nodding to Benny, he turned back to his spreadsheet, taking what solace he could in the vast fortune that had managed to buy him everything but love.

ONE

"Have I ever told you," Peter Shaw asked as he lifted up his flute of champagne, "that you have the most amazing blue eyes?"

"Almost constantly," Lyn Tyrell replied as she straightened the napkins beside the silver tray of canapés. Finished, she glanced over at her coworker and deftly extracted the flute from his grasp before he could take a sip. "The champagne is for the *customers*. Salty spent a lot of money on this promotional party and—"

"I know. I *am* the Guardian's CFO, even if Saltsgaver forgets that little fact from time to time." Peter sounded piqued. "Not one of these expenses was cleared through me."

"I'm sure he just forgot," Lyn said, believing nothing of the sort. As the systems designer lead and Randall Saltsgaver's unofficial right hand, she'd acted as peacemaker between him and Peter more times than she could count. Sometimes she felt like Snow White with the two dwarfs. Three if she counted Jesse. *Funny, I never used to mind their arguments. But lately they've begun to bother me. A lot of things have . . .*

"Well," Peter said with an audible sigh, "If I can't have champagne, at least promise to have a glass with me when this party is over."

Oh Peter, Lyn thought, wishing not for the first time that she could feel something more than friendship for him. A year ago Peter Shaw had been hired away from the Price Waterhouse accounting firm to be Guardian's chief financial officer. He was smart, funny, and handsome enough to make hearts beat faster every time he passed the secretarial pool. Unfortunately, Lyn's heart seemed contrarily immune. "Peter, we've been through all this. I don't believe in dating coworkers—"

"Yes, but women have a habit of changing their minds, particularly when it comes to good-looking, eligible bachelors like me," he said with only a marginal amount of modesty. "In any case, I could probably shake you out of that blue funk you've been in lately."

"I haven't," she replied, but it wasn't the truth. For days she'd had a feeling of impending disaster, as if someone were walking on her grave. She rubbed her arms, feeling cold despite the long sleeves of her white knit dress.

"All right, I have been a bit down lately. It's probably the weather. They're expecting another ice storm later tonight, and more of the same on Friday."

"That's not exactly a news flash in January," he commented drolly. "This is Fort Worth, not Acapulco. What else?"

Self-consciously, she smoothed back a strand of blond hair that had escaped from her elegant bun, wishing she had her vivacious sister Jenny's talent for expressing her feelings. During her youth Lyn had learned to keep her emotions hidden for survival's sake. She found the old habit impossible to break even after she'd been adopted by a loving family, earned a master's degree in computer science, and embarked on a satisfying career with Guardian. Though she tried to stop it, the glass wall she kept between herself and the rest of the world seemed to be growing thicker, taller, stronger.

A year ago she'd gone to a psychiatrist named Dr. Osbourne, who had informed her that she had a problem with trust. Unfortunately, she hadn't been able to tell Lyn how to overcome it.

She sighed, again telling Peter something that was less than the truth. "Well, I've been a *little* concerned about this party, the launch of Guardian's new product line. Frankly, I didn't think Salty's idea of holding it in the Kimbell Art Museum would work. But judging from the turnout," she continued, glancing around at the museum curators, art dealers, and wealthy elite who'd come to view the latest in security technology, "I'd say Guardian Systems is headed for a banner year."

"Lord knows we could use one," Peter replied as he pursed his lips and glanced longingly at the nearby flutes. "Especially if Saltsgaver keeps squandering our profits on caviar and champagne. Heaven only knows what our new employer's going to make of this."

"I heard that!" boomed a nearby voice.

"Salty, you're finally here!" Lyn set down her drink and rushed over to her boss, the man whose showmanship and antics had more than quadrupled Guardian's sales. Randall "Salty" Saltsgaver had made a fortune selling everything from newspapers to high-tech military software, but the turquoise-studded Stetson and string tie he wore with his custom-made tuxedo showed that he was still a country boy at heart. He had the voice of a foghorn, the girth of a linebacker, and the snake-oil style of the proprietor of an old-time medicine show. For the past three years Lyn had alternately been his senior systems designer, his designer lead, his assistant, his confidante, his mother, and his keeper. He was bombastic, egotistical, unrepentantly chauvinistic, and she loved every substantial inch of him.

"Lynnie," he said, engulfing her in a tremendous bear hug. "Honey, you are just about the most beautiful thing this tired old coot has ever laid eyes on. Ain't she the prettiest thing you've ever seen, Shaw?"

Peter's smile turned brittle. "Yes. I think I'll check on the power supply. Jesse was having trouble with it earlier this evening."

"That man is about as friendly as a case of rattlers," Salty commented as he watched Peter walk away.

"He'd be friendlier if you weren't always challenging his figures," Lyn replied archly. "After all, you hired him to be the Guardian's chief financial officer."

"Only 'cause the dag-blamed board of directors forced me to," Salty said, grabbing a handful of finger sandwiches. "And now I've got to kowtow to the new honcho who just bought us."

"Is our new employer here yet?" she asked, glancing at the crowd. "You still haven't told us his name."

"That's the way he wanted it. Said it was publicity, but he's probably just eccentric," Salty complained glumly. "I tell you, Lynnie. Going public was the stupidest thing I ever did."

"It made you a small fortune," she pointed out.

"There's more important things than

money, girl," he said, tipping back his hat. "Say, you're not falling for that stuffed shirt, are you?"

Lyn took a bite of one of the canapés, smiling mischievously. "Why? Are you jealous?"

"Ha! If I were twenty years younger . . ." he replied, flashing the notorious grin that had captured the hearts of three ex-wives and a host of mistresses. "But seriously, Lynnie, he's not right for you. You need a man who makes you laugh and makes you cry, who'll love you so strong and true that you won't have time for nothing 'cept lovin' him back, and maybe giving him a few babies."

Lyn turned away and set her half-empty glass on the table, swallowing the sudden lump in her throat. "That's not very 'nineties' of you, Salty. Nowadays women have both careers and families."

"Some women can do that just fine, but not you. I'd be lost without you, honey, but if the right fella came along," he confessed with a rare show of complete honesty, "I'd fire you quicker than a flea jumps on a hound."

"You are so . . . politically incorrect!"she said in mock censure, giving him a quick, heartfelt hug. As she pulled away she felt a hard shape under his arm, a certain item he'd managed to keep hidden from her during his initial bear hug. "My God!" she whispered, her pretend displeasure turning real. "Salty, you promised me you'd stop carrying that gun."

Salty smiled sheepishly. "I know I did, honey, but—hey, there's Bert Salinger. He wanted me to explain our laser-light security system to him. Gotta go."

"Salty. Salty!" she cried, but her boss had already disappeared into the sea of guests. Politically incorrect doesn't begin to cover it, she thought, her emotions hovering between annoyance and concern. Salty carried a weapon because it was his constitutional right, not because he intended to use it. It was just another way for him to thumb his nose at the "communists, atheists, democrats, and all the other polecats who are doing their level best to run this great country into the ground." Lyn doubted the old man had ever fired his weapon outside of a target range, but the fact that he was carrying it only added to her already considerable sense of uneasiness.

For the next hour, however, she had little time to concentrate on her worries. The curator of a gallery in San Francisco asked her to show him Guardian's new temperature-sensitive alarm system, while a wealthy financier wanted her to explain the old-but-still-very-popular motion-sensor device. She also had several requests to go over the newest addition to the product line, a three-camera identification array that took what amounted to a three-dimensional picture of a valuable item. The picture, which included the item's weight, volume, and spectral analysis, was so incredibly accurate that it made the object virtually impossible to counterfeit—a great deterrent against the steadily increasing black market for fine-art and archaeological forgeries. The Kimbell had already logged several of its prized sculptures into Guardian's security system.

Lyn finally managed to hand the potential clients over to one of her assistants. In need of a break, she scanned the room for a quiet corner, only to find her presence requested by yet another of her coworkers. "Lyn! Over here!"

She swung around, catching sight of Jesse Katz stationed behind the mock-up of the security screen array. Jesse, known as "the one with the earring" by Guardian's more conservative clients, had been hired six months earlier to replace Lyn as senior systems designer when she was promoted to managing lead. He was a genius when it came to cybertechnology. He was also irreverent, tactless, and had a chip on his shoulder the size of Dallas. Lyn suspected that his anger was fueled by the fact that he was too young to be accepted by the scientific community, and too smart to be accepted by his peers. She'd seen the same frustration in her younger brother, Rafe, and her heart went out to Jesse, but that didn't make her excuse his malicious, occasionally destructive behavior. The young man had publicly embarrassed Guardian more than once with his ingenious stunts, and he was only here tonight because he'd given Lyn his word that he'd behave.

That word, however, was in direct contrast to the maniacally mischievous gleam in his eye.

"Jesse," she cautioned sternly as she approached, "remember your promise."

"Chill out. This is harmless." He powered up one of the blank video screens and flipped a complicated array of switches with lightning speed. "Check this out."

For a moment she saw nothing. Then two images appeared at opposite sides of the screen. Lyn recognized the kneeling figure as the Egyptian stone carving of Senenmut, steward of Queen Hatshepsut, and the other as one of the cardsharps from the oil painting of the same name by Caravaggio. Both of them were museum treasures, and both of them had been digitally "photographed" by the array. "No offense, Jesse, but I've already seen these sculptures cataloged."

"Yeah, but have you seen this?" He flipped another switch, looking for all the world like a kid who's just about to set a new record on a video arcade game.

As Lyn bent closer to the screen the figures turned to face each other. Then, incredibly, the limbs of the static sculptures began to move, as if they'd suddenly been brought to life. Swords appeared in their hands and they walked toward each other, engaging in a death-defying battle. Lyn bent closer, delighted and amazed by Jesse's electronic wizardy. "This is incredible. How did you do it?"

"I grabbed the battle pattern from one of those old gladiator movies. I digitized the movements of the actors, then placed the patterns of the art figures on top of them. Once the pattern has been read in, it takes less than a minute to render the whole sequence. Pretty rad, isn't it?"

"I'll say," Lyn agreed as she watched the digitized Senenmut plunge its sword into the heart of the prone sixteenth-century dandy. "Have you shown this to Salty?"

"If he had, I'd have told him to scrap it!"

Lyn spun around and found herself face-to-face with a very angry Salty. "So this is what you've been wasting your time on while you should have been working on the siren sensor."

Jesse glared at his boss. "Cool it, man. The sensor's fine—"

"It just went down in front of the Plano police commissioner!"

"Well, it was fine when I installed it," Jesse claimed defensively, rising to his feet. "You must have screwed it up."

"*I* must have screwed it up. The only time I

screwed up was when I hired a no-account jailbird—"

"I was in a holding cell for twenty-four hours!"

"Guys!" Lyn cried, stepping between them. "Everyone's staring! This is a product launch, not a free-for-all. If you've got to fight, do it in private. Now, Jesse, go and check the laser sensor. And Salty, you try to smooth this over with the customers."

Grumbling and grousing, the two went off to do their respective jobs. Lyn slumped against the video console, feeling drained beyond measure. It wasn't the first time she'd broken up a fight between her boss and the company's whiz kid, and she doubted it would be the last. But suddenly the whole thing seemed so pointless, so incredibly futile. Next year she'd still be breaking up fights between them, and the next, and the next. *What am I doing with my life? What the hell am I doing?*

"Champagne?"

She turned her head and saw Peter standing at her side, sipping from one of the forbidden flutes and holding another out to her. What the hell, she thought as she took the offered glass. "What would I do without you?"

"Why bother to find out? Go out with me."

It wasn't the first time he'd asked, but it was the first time that Lyn seriously considered it.

She wasn't attracted to Peter—at least, not the head-over-heels, earth-moving, soul-shaking kind of attraction—but she did care about him. More important, she trusted him. With Peter she felt a sense of security. Maybe love wasn't that crucial.

The pragmatic side of her argued that security and companionship were adequate foundations for a good relationship. She thought about her adopted parents Luke and Sarah Tyrell, and about the deep, true love they shared, even after a decade of marriage. But she'd seen enough relationships to know that theirs was the exception rather than the norm. *Maybe I'm one of those people who doesn't need to be in love to have a happy marriage. Maybe I'm one of those people who can't fall in love.*

You did once. . . .

She slammed down the memory, locking it away like a shuttered room that contains both treasures and monsters. Salty might say that she needed love, but the only thing it had ever brought her was pain, despair, and a loneliness as black as a starless night. *I don't want to go through that again.*

She set her champagne flute on the console and turned to face him. "All right," she said quietly. "I'll go out with you."

"I knew you'd come to your senses," Peter exclaimed, ignoring the people around them as he took her in his arms. "You won't regret it. I'll give you everything you ever wanted."

Not quite, she thought as she resigned herself to the embrace. *You can't make me forget.* She closed her eyes, willing away the memories of a boy with hair the color of dark gold and a spirit as free and wild as the Texas sky. *I've got to put it behind me. I've got to get on with my life.*

Resolved, she rested her chin on Peter's shoulder and tightened her arms around him, knowing that she was doing the right thing, the mature thing, the only thing she could do under the circumstances. She couldn't bear living this half-life anymore—she had to free herself from the shadows of her past and break down the glass wall that separated her from the rest of the world. Encouraged by the fact that she'd finally made a choice to change her life, she opened her eyes and lifted her gaze to Peter's —only to find he wasn't looking at her, but at something past her shoulder.

"I don't believe it," he said in an awed voice. "Lyn, guess who just walked in."

She stepped out of Peter's arms and turned around, scanning the close-packed crowd that filled the main room. "Governor Bush?"

"No. Someone much more important," he said, pointing to the far end of the room. "A *major* player."

Lyn craned her neck, trying to see who Peter was talking about. Whoever it was had certainly impressed him—enough to drive their possible romance out of his mind. More curious than annoyed, she cast her gaze once more over the sea of glittering party goers . . . and ran aground on a rugged profile she'd never expected to see again. *It wasn't. It couldn't be. It—*

The man turned, grinning with killer charm at the elderly woman beside him. God, it is Curt. I'd know that smile anywhere.

Seven years collapsed into a minute. Always tall, he'd grown leaner over the years, and his powerful form radiated the confidence of a man who'd spent most of his life working outdoors. With maturity he'd acquired a veneer of social elegance, but she'd have given odds that he could strip off that veneer as easily as he could shed that impeccably tailored tuxedo. Underneath the elegance he was still the same hell-raising cowboy who'd held the three-county record for bull riding, who'd ridden his horse flat out in a driving rain to rescue a lost calf, and who'd spent a golden summer letting her teach him about assets and liabilities, while he taught her about love. . . .

Her thoughts ended abruptly as Peter yanked her forward into the crowd. "Come on. Let's get to him before the rest of the crowd finds out he's here. Maybe we'll pick up a few pointers. They say that everything he touches turns to gold."

Not everything, she thought, feeling the strange uneasiness within her build to a crescendo. She was over him, she reminded herself. She'd been over him for years. But that didn't stop her from remembering how deeply she'd loved him.

Or remembering how coldly he'd broken her young and trusting heart.

Curt wondered how he was going to get away from the elderly woman with blue hair without either hurting her feelings or dying of boredom—when he saw Benny Fortuna striding through the assembled guests like a tank in a tuxedo. *Salvation!*

"Sorry, ma'am, but I see my assistant heading this way," he said as he gave the woman his most charmingly apologetic smile. "You know what they say—business before pleasure."

"Oh, of course," she said as she released her hold on his arm, blushing like a schoolgirl under his melting grin. "Maybe I'll see you later?"

"Absolutely," he lied as he walked away, wincing from the twinge of a conscience that should have been dead and buried long ago.

"You're Curt Brennermen, aren't you?" a man's voice behind him said, just as Benny reached him.

"Unfortunately," Curt muttered as he

watched his plans for a quick getaway vanish like a puff of smoke. He turned to the man behind him, sizing him up in less than a second. Ivy League. Cushy desk job. Probably hadn't done a day's hard labor in his entire life.

"Peter Shaw," the man said, giving Curt's hand what he thought was a forceful shake. "It's an honor to have you here at our gala."

"Your gala?"

"Yes, I work for Guardian. I hope you're having a good time."

"Wonderful," Curt said, gazing longingly toward the front entrance hall. "But I'm late for another . . . appointment. Nice meeting you, Mr. Shaw."

He started to turn away, but Shaw called him back. "Please, there's a coworker of mine who'd like to meet you. She'll be here in a— there she is."

Sighing, Curt looked around, steeling himself to meet yet another blue-haired old lady. But the lady in question was neither blue-haired nor old. She also wasn't a stranger. Years ago he'd given up any hope of seeing her again. Yet here she was, walking toward him like something out of a dream.

She was more polished than he remembered, and the elegantly simple white wool dress she wore hugged curves far more womanly than the ones he recalled. Yet she still moved with the same coltish grace that had always fascinated him, and her hair, though now pulled back in a sophisticated bun, still reminded him of spun moonlight.

"Hello, Curt," she said quietly.

Her voice was the same, yet not the same. She still spoke with the soft lilt that reminded him of a mockingbird's song, but the years had added confidence to her word and her bearing, giving her an almost regal air. The shy farm girl he'd known had blossomed into a lovely and intelligent woman, and he admired her for it. "Hello, Lyn. It's been a long time."

"You *know* each other?" Peter exclaimed.

Curt nodded, drinking in the sight of her face like a parched man tasting water. "Lyn and I grew up in the same east Texas county. We were—"

"Neighbors," she blurted out. "We were *neighbors.*"

A muscle in Curt's jaw pulled taut. Seven years had gone by and she still didn't trust him. "I was going to say we were friends," he said with lethal softness. "We were friends once. Or am I wrong about that too?"

Her confident demeanor slipped. For a heart-stopping moment he saw the face of the girl he'd loved all those years ago, whose cornflower-blue eyes still haunted his dreams—

A siren shriek cut the air.

"Damn, Jesse's got the volume turned up again," Lyn said, wincing. "I'd better get it straightened out." She glanced at Curt and hesitated, looking for an instant as if she wanted to say more. But instead she shook her head wordlessly and disappeared into the crowd.

"I'm sorry, Mr. Brennermen," Shaw apologized. "She's usually not that abrupt. I'm sure she'll be back. Meanwhile, if you'd care to look at some of our products—"

"Not right now," Curt said brusquely, his eyes still focused on the place where she'd disappeared. Tough choices were part of his business. She'd been one of them. A smart man would leave it there.

But the truth was, Curt had never been particularly smart where Lyn was concerned. He turned to Benny. "Wait for me by the door. I'll be back. Mr. Shaw, if you'll excuse me . . ."

Without waiting for an answer, he started off through the crowd, scanning the sea of faces for a pair of cornflower-blue eyes. He didn't know what he was going to say to her when he found her, he didn't even know what he wanted to say. But he knew he had to see her once more before he left.

Years of despair and disillusionment had stripped away most of his once sacred beliefs, but one remained. Even his bitterest enemies acknowledged that Curt Brennermen was a man who paid his debts. And he owed Lyn Tyrell an apology that was six years overdue.

TWO

You're a coward, Lyn Tyrell, an inner voice accused as she strode down the empty hallway toward the back gallery. *A dyed-in-the-wool, lily-livered coward.* And the fact that she'd spent most of her life meeting and besting her challenges didn't make a damn bit of difference.

After she'd finished with Jesse, she'd told him she was going to the gallery to check on the museum's working model of the three-camera security array. But that was only an excuse. Truth was, she was running away from the party. Truth was, she'd have run to the other side of the world if she could.

She entered the deserted gallery, feeling like a powder keg about to explode. "Damn you, Curt Brennermen," she muttered to the empty plaster walls. "Damn you for coming back to Texas, and for showing up at my company's gala, and for looking so god-awful handsome—"

She rubbed her aching temples, realizing she was rambling like an idiot. Curt had every right to visit his home state. He was also perfectly free to show up at Guardian's gala—which, as Peter had pointed out, was a compliment to their company.

The shock on Curt's face had told her that he hadn't expected to see her any more than she'd expected to see him. And as for being handsome—well, that wasn't his fault, any more than the smoldering ache in her middle that started every time she looked at him was hers.

It wasn't fair. But, as her mother Sarah always said, "Fair is where you take your hogs to win blue ribbons." Sighing, she walked over to the equipment and stepped into the circle of posts that were mounted with sophisticated video cameras. In the center of the array stood the pedestal where the art was placed for cataloging. Currently it held a small Remington bronze, a statue of a cowboy trying his damnedest to stay on the back of a bucking horse.

She ran her finger gently along the edge of the statue, smiling sadly. She felt a certain kinship with the brave little rider. *You can hang on for seconds, fella. Maybe a whole minute. But eventually that bronc is going to send you flying. You can't hang on forever, any more than I can ride out the wild memories in my own mind.*

Lyn's early life was not something she was proud of. Her biological mother had been a pretty woman who'd believed her face and figure entitled her to more than life had seen fit to give her. Regina Foster had complained bitterly to the people who cared about her, eventually driving them all away, until the only one left was her young daughter. The sole witness of her mother's tirades, Lyn had learned to shut out unpleasant reality by curling up with a book and entering her own little world of wonderful dreams. Her mother had called her lazy and stupid, but Lyn knew better. She knew that the stalwart knights and heroes of the stories existed somewhere. All she had to do was wait for one of them to rescue her.

Her life took an unexpected turn when she was twelve and her mother married again. Her new stepfather had enough money to allow her mother to stop working, but Lyn was afraid of him. He was always looking at her strangely and hugging her too tightly.

One night he came into her bedroom and touched her in a way that made her feel dirty. She told her mother, but Regina didn't believe her—or didn't want to believe her. She'd told Lyn's stepfather, but the man had denied it. Later, he'd taken the girl aside and slapped her so hard, it cut her lip, telling her to keep her mouth shut or else. The look in his eyes made her blood turn to ice. That night she'd run away.

The little money she'd had was soon gone. She'd lived on the streets, scavenging like a rat for food and shelter. She'd seen acts of horrible cruelty and selfless generosity—learning more about human nature in four months than most people do in a lifetime. In the end the police caught her, but that had only extended the nightmare. She found that after she'd left, her mother and stepfather had argued constantly. The fights had turned violent, and a few weeks before, her mother had been brought into the hospital, shot through the heart.

For a long time Lyn blamed herself. If she hadn't run away she might have been able to prevent it, and her mother might still be alive. It took a dedicated child-welfare lawyer to finally convince the young girl that her stepfather's sickness was to blame and that it had nothing to do with her. The lawyer's name was Sarah Gallegher, and she eventually adopted Lyn and took her to live with her other "problem children" at Corners, her east Texas farm.

Lyn was a shy, awkward nineteen-year-old who was still dealing with her troubled past when Curt came into her life. He was the hell-raising son of Sam Brennermen, the richest man in the county. Most people were afraid of Curt, and with good reason—the man was a powder keg just waiting for a match. He'd been thrown out of two colleges and was going to be thrown out of a third if his grades didn't improve. It was the general opinion of the local gossips that he was bad to the bone, well past redemption.

Lyn had agreed with them, until she'd looked beneath his tough, defensive exterior and found a heart of pure gold. She'd waited all her life for a knight in shining armor to come to her, and the fact that his armor was tarnished had made her love him all the more. She'd loved him with all the stored-up passion in her dreamer's soul. And she'd paid dearly for it.

"Lyn."

The rough baritone voice called her back to the present, breaking apart her fragile memories like a shattered Christmas-tree ornament. She stiffened, steeling her heart against feelings that should have been laid to rest years ago, which until tonight she'd sworn she *had* laid to rest. Trust Curt Brennermen to come up on her blind side.

"Aren't you going to be missed?" she asked without turning around.

"Benny's running interference for me. He'll keep the reporters off my trail until I get back. I think he enjoys it," he said, his tone rich with laughter. But the laughter disappeared in his next statement. "I need to talk with you."

Need. How did he always know which words would strike straight to her heart? Once again she shored up her crumbling defenses, and made a show of typing a series of numbers into the computer console. "I'm busy right now, but if you stop by my office Monday, I'm sure—"

"Can't you even look at me, Angel?"

Her hands froze on the keypad. "You have no right to call me that."

"Turn around and tell me to my face."

His words were both a challenge and a command. Either way, she couldn't deny it. She turned around slowly, reluctant to face him, yet unable not to. It happened seven years ago, she thought. Seven long years.

Seven years collapsed into a minute when she saw him. Alone, without the distracting crowd around him, she felt the full force of his presence. The silence of the gallery wrapped around them like a shared secret, drawing her into the midnight darkness of his eyes. He stared at her with an intensity that made her feel hot and cold all at once. She could cut the memories out of her mind, but not her body. Please, not again.

"You haven't changed," he said, giving her his devastating smile.

I'm not buying it, Brennermen. Not this time.

"What do you want, Curt? To relive old conquests?"

A slight tightening of his jaw was the only indication that her barb had struck home. "You were never just a conquest. Don't belittle what we had—"

"*I* didn't belittle it. You were the one who ended our relationship. You were the one who sent the 'Dear Lyn' letter."

"I had my reasons," he said grimly.

"Fine. And I've got mine for asking you to get the hell out of here!"

"Damn," he cursed, plowing his hands through his dark gold mane. "Can't we have a civil conversation? What's wrong with us? We were friends once."

We were more than friends, she thought bleakly. We were two people who shared the same heart. We were so much in love that we forgot that the rest of the world mattered. I would have died for you, and you tossed me out like yesterday's leftovers.

"What is it you want?" she repeated, exhausted in a way she hadn't been in years.

"What I want," he said through gritted teeth, "is to apologize."

She stared at him as if her soul were a dishtowel he'd just wrung dry. For years she'd imagined a meeting between them, turning the possible conversations over and over in her mind. She'd calculated perfect responses to everything he might say to her—except an apology.

He had no right to expect her forgiveness. No right at all. She turned back to the keyboard. "Okay, you've apologized. Good-bye."

Now he was the one who looked surprised. "That's all?"

"What more do you want?" she asked sharply. *Dammit, this isn't like me. I'm not a vindictive person.*

Dr. Osbourne had warned her that she hadn't fully dealt with the pain of the breakup. Now, faced with the man who'd caused it, she realized how right her psychiatrist had been. She was acting like a child—a shrewish, petulant child. It wasn't the way she wanted to behave. It wasn't the way she wanted him to remember her. "I'm sorry. It's been . . . a long day."

"And I didn't make it any easier by showing up out of the blue."

"No," she acknowledged with a resigned sigh. "You didn't."

The corner of his hard mouth lifted in a reluctant smile. It was a look she'd seen dozens of times on his younger, less cynical face, and the memory of it ached her heart. For the first time she wondered what his life had been like during these last six years. His letters from South America had made the place sound like a jungle paradise, a kind of Marriott resort for

Tarzan. According to the articles she'd read about him, he had everything a man could want, but there was no mistaking the lines of strain around his mouth, or the shadows under his eyes. *Don't kid yourself, Lyn. He's probably exhausted because he's been partying all night.*

He glanced at the ceiling, then shook his head and gave a slow, weary laugh. "Ah, Lyn," he said as he stuck his hands inelegantly into the elegant pockets of his tuxedo pants, "of all the companies in all the world, why did I have to walk into yours?"

She couldn't resist a smile at the deliberate misquoting of Humphrey Bogart's *Casablanca* dialogue. "Just lucky I guess."

His mouth twitched higher. He came closer, his shoes sounding hard and hollow against the marble floor. Lord, I'm lost, she thought, feeling her heart begin to shatter all over again.

"I know we can't be friends, but at least let's not be enemies." He took his hand from his pocket and offered it to her.

She looked at his large, worked-roughened hand as if it were a rattler. She didn't want to shake hands with him. The thought of touching him in any way . . . But it seemed that good manners were as hard to give up as bad vices. Cautiously, warily, she extended her hand toward his. "I suppose it makes no difference. After tonight we won't be seeing each other again, and—why are you looking at me like that?"

"That's not exactly true. I know Saltsgaver told you that you've got a new owner. Well," he said as his dark gaze met hers, "you're looking at him."

"You can't own us," she cried in undisguised horror as she drew back her hand. "Guardian's too small to interest you. I've read what kind of companies you buy. Huge conglomerates. Multinational corporations."

"Those are the ones that make the news. I also buy small companies with big potential. Guardian's one of those," he told her as he rubbed his chin, giving her a ghost of a grin. "Actually, you should be thanking me. Considering the state of this company's finances, I'm the best thing that could have happened to it."

"Yeah, like the butcher's the best thing to happen to a cow," she shot back. Having Curt Brennermen in charge of the company she'd helped nurture into existence was like putting a wolf in charge of a flock of sheep. Except that wolves attacked out of hunger—he did it for sport. "Sorry, but I'm too much of a rancher's daughter to believe that."

"You're also a businesswoman. I can make something of this company, but I'm going to need the support of you and your associates.

Otherwise I'm starting from degree zero. I'm going to need your . . . trust."

She couldn't believe he'd said that. Not after . . . "You've got to be kidding. I'd sooner trust a rattlesnake. And that's exactly what I'm going to tell my associates, Mr. Brennermen. Now, if you'll excuse me, I've got a presentation to give—while I'm still employed."

She started to push past him, but he grabbed her wrist, holding her back. "God knows I've made mistakes, but I've tried to make up for them. Everyone else is willing to judge me by the good things I've done as well as the bad. Everyone except you, Angel."

"Don't call me that," she said, but the protest rang hollow even to her ears. Being so close to him called up memories she'd spent more than half a decade forgetting. She smelled his essence beneath the expensive cologne, felt the iron strength of his fingers, saw the tempering gentleness in the depths of his midnight eyes. She shut out the memories, filling her consciousness with production schedules, arithmetic equations, grocery lists. But even as her mind rejected the memories her body remembered. And it pulled toward him like the tide is pulled toward the land.

She wanted to believe in him—so much that it frightened her. The need to trust rose up inside her and beat against the glass barrier that she'd erected against the rest of the world.

A few more hits would shatter it completely. She'd be free of it at last, free of the half-life she'd been living. Free . . .

Like a wary doe she raised her eyes, looking at him without the protection of her mistrust. Maturity had hardened him, giving him the rough-hewn, slightly battered look of a man who'd weathered many battles and intended to weather a good many more. A small knot on the blade of his nose showed that at least some of those battles had been physical. She found herself wondering about the fights, and feeling a strange regret that she hadn't been there when he'd needed comfort. It was all she could do not to reach up and smooth her finger along the old wound.

But it was his eyes more than anything that spoke of the change in him. Always passionate, they blazed with the power of a man who'd learned how to reach out and grasp life, and shape it the way he wanted. A man who'd learned to take what he wanted and damn the consequences.

A man who'd promised to marry her, then tossed her aside.

She drew back, shocked by how close she'd come to letting herself believe that he'd changed. Tigers didn't change their stripes, rattler's didn't change their diamonds. "I can't help you, Curt," she said, her words pouring out in a rush. "You'll have my resignation

Monday morning. I can't work for you. Not now. Not ever."

She pulled away and he let her go, releasing her as if all the strength had gone out of him. She left the gallery, but paused at the door, as if she couldn't quite shake the force that drew them together. She looked back, and saw that he hadn't moved—hadn't even turned to watch her go. He stood with one hand on the computer monitor, his shoulders bent in a weariness she'd never expected to see in a man so vital. He looked like a once proud lion who'd lost the will to hunt. She swallowed a sudden knot in her throat, then turned and ran like a frightened rabbit down the hall. Only it wasn't Curt she was afraid of. It was what might happen if she let herself go back into the gallery.

Still running, she glanced back, half dreading, half hoping—and ran full tilt into Salty.

"Hell, Lynnie, where's the fire?" he said, steadying her.

"I'm sorry, I—Salty!" she cried, remembering what she'd just been told. "Something terrible's happened. Curt Brennermen's the man who bought Guardian. We've got to—"

"I know."

"You know," she said, marveling at his un-Salty-like calm. "Then why aren't you mad as hell? I am."

He scratched his chin, his eyes displaying the shrewdness that he normally hid behind his bombastic exterior. "Lynnie, there's things going on you don't know about."

Lyn's emotions were already badly frayed. She was in no mood to play twenty questions. "Look, if something's up I think I have a right to—"

Her words were drowned out by a loud siren blast.

"Damn," she cried, covering her ears, "Jesse's turned up the volume again." She swiveled toward the siren and saw that Peter was already at the instrument panel, apparently turning down the noise as he explained the features of the security system to a group of curious customers. Some of the customers were a few feet away from Salty and her, well within earshot. She dropped her voice, knowing that any word of Curt's purchase of Guardian would go through the crowd like wildfire. "Maybe we shouldn't go into this right now."

"Smart thinking," her boss agreed as he glanced in the direction of the crowd, looking like a thundercloud about to burst. After a second he turned back to Lyn. "I'll tell you this, Lyn. If what that sidewinding snake told me is true, Brennermen and I have a lot to talk about."

Guess I'm not the only one who's discovered Curt's true nature, she thought as she nodded toward the far gallery. "The sidewinding snake's in there, if you want to talk with him."

Salty looked puzzled. "Who?"

"Brennermen, of course. He's in the far gallery with the computer array. And I suggest you take along a vial of snake-venom antidote. The man's pure poison."

For a long moment Salty stared at her, completely perplexed. Then his brow suddenly lit with understanding and he smiled, chucking her under the chin as if she were a young child. "You see me later, Lynnie. I think you and I have a lot to talk about as well."

She would have asked what he meant, but at that moment Peter called her to come over to help with the display. By the time she looked back, Salty had already disappeared into the far gallery.

For the next half hour Lyn hardly had time to breathe, much less think about her encounter with Curt. Between equipment adjustments and customer questions she was practically run off her feet. She told herself more than once that she was being foolish—that any sales she made would benefit a company owned by Brennermen. But she'd spent too many years thinking of Guardian's employees as her second family to do anything to harm them now. The thought of leaving the job she loved cast even more gloom on an already dismal evening.

"Christ, Lyn, if your jaw was any lower it'd be scraping the floor."

"Flattery like that will get you nowhere, Jesse," she commented as she turned around to face her less-than-gallant coworker. "Especially since I just had to turn down that siren of yours again. You promised not to turn the volume up."

"I didn't. Honest. But it's not a bad idea. This whole corporate party trip is making me nauseous," he said, his smile as bright as the diamond in his ear. "Tell you what. Why don't you and I blow this Popsicle stand?"

"Leave? Jesse, we can't do that."

"I'll say you can't," Peter agreed, appearing at her side. "The customers are bombarding me with questions. And that strongman Brennermen brought with him is roaming through the crowd like a rogue elephant."

"Where is Curt, anyway?" Lyn asked as she scanned the crowd, trying her best to sound nonchalant.

Peter shrugged. "I haven't seen him or Salty for some time. Maybe they've left already."

Lyn shook her head. "Curt wouldn't leave without his bodyguard. And besides, Salty said he was going to talk with me later."

"About what?" they asked in unison.

Great, Lyn thought. The last thing she wanted to do was tell the two about Curt's takeover of Guardian. Jesse was already primed for one of his notorious temper tantrums. Peter's displeasure would be more subtle, but he'd be cold as ice to everyone he talked with, including the customers. "It's kind of complicated," she said, using as much of the truth as she dared. "Anyway, I'm sure Salty will tell you himself as soon as he—"

A woman's scream split the air. Lyn's words froze on her lips, and for a single moment the gaudy, glittering crowd froze with her. Then the whole room erupted into chaos.

"What happened?"

"Was someone electrocuted?"

"Should someone call the police?"

The questions rained down with the force of a hailstorm. Peter and Jesse pushed their way through the crowd, leaving Lyn to field most of the verbal barrage. She did her best to placate the customers, wishing like hell that Salty would come out and roar the crowd to silence. Gradually she worked her way forward toward the heart of the turmoil, which seemed to be centered near the far gallery at the end of the hallway. She was making good progress down the hallway when someone grabbed her elbow, holding her back.

"You don't want to go in there," Benny stated.

"Why not?" she asked, as surprised by the big man's statement as she was by his actions.

"You just don't," he said with deadly certainty.

She twisted sideways, pulling out of his grip. Determined, she forced her way through the crowd, needing to see what Benny had tried to shield her from. She refused to speculate, she didn't dare consider, but when she squeezed herself through the crowded doorway to the gallery, she saw that her worst fears had come true.

Salty wouldn't be talking to her or anyone else again. His motionless body lay facedown near the computer console, a dark stain pooling on the floor around him.

THREE

"Thank you for waiting, Ms. Tyrell," said the policewoman as she ushered Lyn into the small museum office that had been commandeered for the questioning process. "This won't take long."

Lyn nodded numbly and took a seat. It had been a long time since she'd sat in front of a police officer for questioning—the last time had been when her mother had died. She'd matured twenty years since that night, yet the feelings she was experiencing were horribly familiar—emptiness, frustration, and the nagging guilt that somehow she could have prevented this from happening. If she'd made Salty take off his gun, if she'd kept a closer eye on him . . .

"I was probably one of the last people to see him alive," she confessed without being asked. "I've tried to think of someone who might want to . . . to do this to him, but—"

"Ms. Tyrell, I don't need information on Mr. Saltsgaver," the officer interrupted as she efficiently flipped open her notepad. "What I do need is anything you can tell me about Curt Brennermen."

"Curt? Why would you want to know about him? Unless, oh God—" she breathed, gripping the arms of her chair in terror. If someone was insane enough to murder Salty, they might be crazy enough to—

"Please," she said, dropping her voice to a harsh whisper. "Please, is he all right?"

"As far as we know," the older woman assured her. "I understand from some of the other guests that you and Mr. Brennermen knew each other. From your reaction just now, I assume that relationship was . . . close."

"We were lovers," Lyn said bluntly, knowing the police could find out easily enough if they wanted to. "Several years ago, while I was in my junior year of college. He lived in the same east Texas county that I did. The relationship didn't last long. His father died suddenly of a heart attack. Shortly afterward he took a job in a South American oil field. We wrote each other for about a year, then . . ." She smoothed back her hair, suddenly feeling as awkward as she had when she was a teenager. "I didn't see him again . . . until to-night."

"So he left you," the officer stated in a *Dragnet* monotone.

Lyn stiffened. She was uncomfortable enough about the past without having it thrown in her face by this Joe Friday clone. "You're supposed to be trying to find out who killed Salty."

"That *is* what I'm trying to find out, Ms. Tyrell. You see, no one has seen Mr. Brennermen since Mr. Saltsgaver's body was found." She leaned toward Lyn and added, "Mr. Saltsgaver's gun also cannot be located."

Lyn sat back in her chair, stunned by what the woman was suggesting. "You think that Curt shot Salty with his own gun and . . ." She shook her head, wanting to laugh at the absurdity of the thought. "Look, I'm no fan of Brennermen, but I can tell you right now that he didn't kill anyone. He couldn't. He's not that kind of man."

The policewoman bent to jot a remark on her notepad. "Last year I investigated the case of a man who claimed his wife had left him five years earlier. We eventually found her buried in his garden under his prizewinning rose-bushes. Everybody said he wasn't 'that kind of man' either."

Lyn opened her mouth to reply, but the words died on her tongue. The policewoman's words of warning didn't convince her that Curt was Salty's killer, but they did remind her how little she knew about the man. She recalled the moment in the gallery when she'd looked into his eyes, and saw a stranger staring back at her. The Curt Brennermen she'd know seven years ago hadn't been capable of killing anyone. But seven years was a long time.

She recalled Salty's anger when he'd been on his way to see Curt. Perhaps there'd been a scuffle, and . . . "No, I still don't buy it. If there was a fight and the gun accidentally went off, Curt wouldn't have run. Whatever else he is, he's is no coward."

The woman looked up sharply. "We don't believe it was an accident, Ms. Tyrell. Mr. Saltsgaver was shot in the back—which does not suggest an impassioned fight. Also, we understand that Mr. Brennermen has a reputation for 'skirting' the law. His right-hand man also has a criminal record."

"Lots of people have records," Lyn stated. "Lord, even I have a record. I was picked up for vagrancy as a kid."

"Mr. Fortuna's crimes are a little more serious," the woman stated, her impartial monotone annoying. "In addition, one of your co-employees—I can't mention the name for privacy reasons—told us that Saltsgaver believed someone on the inside was planning to sell Guardian's technological secrets to the Mafia."

"That's ridiculous! Our product security is airtight. This person must have been mistaken."

"Perhaps," the officer mused. "But this person also said that Saltsgaver found this out shortly before the sale to Brennermen's holding company was final."

"It's still only hearsay," Lyn said, wondering why she was so eager to defend a man she was supposed to despise. "You have no concrete evidence."

"I'm afraid we do." The woman turned around and switched on the computer console behind her. "This digital recording was taken off your company's demonstration security system—the one you call the 'matrix array.' I think you ought to take a look at it."

The picture on the monochrome screen was grainy and indistinct, like a television set whose signal keeps fading in and out. Problems with the power feed, Lyn thought automatically, making a mental note to inform Jesse. Her concern with the picture quality dissolved, however, when she realized where the recording had taken place. "That's the back gallery, isn't it. I recognize the Remington—"

Words froze in her throat as she saw two figures enter the camera's field. They moved like stick figures, their actions sharp and jerky due to the poor quality of the recording. Nevertheless, it was impossible to mistake the identity of the two people, or the deadly intent of their actions. Curt and Salty were fighting like a couple of bloodthirsty street thugs. She watched almost hypnotized as Curt pulled Salty's gun from its holster, toppled him backward on the floor, and calmly shot him in the back.

Lyn jerked in her chair, feeling the shot go through her own heart.

The policewoman switched off the computer console. "We wanted to keep this evidence out of media hands, at least until we can apprehend Brennermen. We've got an APB out on him now. His family and most of his known associates are being watched, but we don't have enough resources to cover everyone. Because of your past relationship, he may try to get in touch with you."

"I doubt it," Lyn said, still staring at the blank screen. "We haven't been close for a long time. I really don't know him anymore." *If I ever did.*

"Well, if he does, please contact me or your local law-enforcement office immediately. He's a dangerous man." The officer snapped her notebook shut and handed Lyn her card. Then, in an unexpected show of compassion, she covered the younger woman's hand with her own. "I know what a shock this must be for you."

I doubt it, Lyn thought. It didn't pay to trust people. It certainly didn't pay to love them. She lifted her head, her words hollowly precise. "If Curt Brennermen does try to contact me, I'll inform you immediately. Now, if you don't mind, I'd like to get out of here."

The night had turned bitterly cold. The parking lot of the Kimbell was empty as a tomb, the sodium lights casting a ghostly glow on the ice-sheeted asphalt and on the pale steel body of the police car that crawled through the deserted lot. In the passenger seat Lyn pulled her coat collar close around her neck, shivering more from the graveyard images than from the cold. Salty was dead and Curt was suspected by the police of being his murderer. She felt like she'd stepped into her worst nightmare.

"You sure you don't want me to drive you home?" the officer beside her asked.

"Thanks," she said gruffly, trying to sound appreciative. It wasn't the young man's fault that he'd been ordered to drive her to her car, when the only thing she really wanted was to be alone. At least most of the guests, along with her coworkers, had already been sent home. She didn't want to talk with anyone right now, even Peter. She wanted to climb into her solitude and wrap it around her, and try to forget the horror that had taken place barely two hours ago. Salty was dead and Curt was his murderer. She'd watched him pull the trigger.

"Is that your car?"

Lyn looked up, surprised that they'd already driven around to the back of the museum. But there was her trusty royal-blue Jeep Cherokee, parked right next to the back Dumpster. And parked right next to it was . . . She blinked back tears as she looked at Salty's white Cadillac. *Dammit, I can't start crying. If I do, I'll never stop.*

The young officer opened his glove compartment and pulled out a box of tissues. "My mom makes me carry these. They come in handy . . . unfortunately." He handed one to Lyn, looking uncertain. "I wouldn't mind driving you—"

Suddenly the radio squawked, spitting out a stream of unintelligible numbers. They made no sense to Lyn, but the officer's spine went rigid. "Sorry, lady, there's been a robbery— look, I can still take you—"

"No, you go on," she said as she quickly opened the car door and stepped out. She waved to the officer, tissue still clutched in her hand. "And tell your mom thanks, okay?"

She watched him go, his tires crunching against the hard-packed ice as he drove away. She waited until the sound had faded, leaving behind only the silence of the winter night. She breathed it in like a living thing, grateful finally to be alone. At least, she thought, this nightmare evening is almost over—

A shadow fell across her. She spun around, opening her mouth to scream like hell, but the sound caught in her throat. The last person in the world she expected to see stood in front of her, his tuxedo collar pulled up inadequately against the bitter wind.

"Curt," she breathed, more relieved than she'd thought possible to see him. "You didn't run after all. But you've got to get back in there. There's been some kind of crazy mistake. The police think you—"

Her words died as she saw the gun dangling from his right hand. She knew that the nightmare hadn't ended.

It had only just begun.

FOUR

Her gaze riveted on the gun. "You killed him," she whispered in horror. "You actually—"

She whirled around and started running across the parking lot, praying she wouldn't slip on the ice. She didn't get far. Before she'd gone a dozen steps, he caught her wrist and turned her to face him, binding both her arms to her sides in a viselike grip. "Dammit, Lyn, you run on this ice in those heels and you'll break your neck."

"You're concerned for my safety?" she croaked, holding back an obscene urge to laugh. "That's great, coming from a *murderer*."

The word lashed him. His eyes darkened, boring into her with the intensity of a man hovering on the edge of madness. He tightened his grip on her arms and pulled her up, lifting her almost off the ground so that her gaze met his squarely. "I thought you were the one person . . . Ah hell. I didn't kill Saltsgaver," he said, speaking every word with the force of a hammer blow. "I'm innocent."

She glanced at the gun stuck into the waistband of his cummerbund. He outweighed her. He outgunned her. It was time to try a new tack. "Of course you are," she said, smiling weakly. "And if you'll put me down, we can go back to the police and—"

"Stop it," he hissed, his grip tightening mercilessly. "Don't lie to me. You think I did it. But I swear to you I didn't. Someone hit me from behind and knocked me out, and when I woke up—ow!"

He yelped with surprise as she kicked him in the shins. Seizing the moment, she twisted in his grip, struggling like a fighting cat to break free. "Help me! Somebody help—"

Cold metal pressed against the side of her throat, freezing her into immobility. For a long moment the only sounds in the silent world were the howl of the rising wind and the deafening tattoo of her heart beating against her ribs. Then he spoke.

"It appears I have two choices," he commented as calmly as if he were telling her the time. "I can shoot you, like you think I shot Salty. Or I can take you with me. Which would you prefer?"

She swallowed, finding the small gesture

unusually difficult with a gun barrel held against her throat. "Curt, if you give yourself up, they might—"

"Choose," he demanded, pressing the gun deeper into her flesh. "Choose, or I'll choose for you."

Bastard! She wanted to scream at him, to fight and fight until she was too exhausted to remember the horror of seeing Salty's body lying facedown on the floor in the gallery, or the despair she'd felt when she'd seen the tape of Curt coldly shooting him through the heart. If she had any kind of courage she would have yelled out at the top of her lungs, and taken the consequences. But she discovered, at this eleventh hour, that she was just too fond of living to risk it. "I'll . . . go with you."

He bent down, so close that she could feel his hot breath searing her sensitive ear. "Say please."

"What! I'm not going to—" She gasped as his iron fingers bit into her arm. She'd forgotten how strong he was, how he used to wrestle full-grown steers to the ground. Even without the gun she was no match for him. She closed her eyes, feeling what little courage she had left drain out of her. "Please."

She could almost feel him smile.

He yanked her around and herded her back toward her Cherokee. "Unfortunately we'll have to take your car. Benny drove off in mine an hour ago."

"Too bad you didn't go with him," she muttered.

His chuckle surprised her. "Believe me, I wanted to, but the police were swarming around him like flies." He dropped his voice, sounding almost apologetic as he added, "If it makes you feel any better, you weren't my first choice of escape route."

"It doesn't," she replied sharply, glancing up at him.

Their gazes locked. She looked up into the night darkness of his eyes, and felt chilled to the bone. There was no mercy in those eyes, no remorse. They burned with a cold, contained fire, a strange energy that seemed to suck all the life and strength and hope from her body. She shivered, but not from the cold. Years ago she'd heard people speak of the demons that rode Curt's soul. This was the first time she'd actually seen one.

Suddenly she was almost more afraid for him than for herself. "Curt, don't do this," she pleaded. "You've got to give yourself up. If you don't, guilt over Salty's murder will eat you alive. I know you didn't mean to do it, even if the tape makes it look like you—"

"What tape?"

"The tape of the murder. The police took it from the security computer array in the gallery. It . . ." She hesitated, oddly unwilling to say the rest. "It pretty much convicts you."

He arched an eyebrow. "Does it, now?"

She expected him to be devastated by the news that the police had the murder on film. Instead, he seemed almost amused. "Yes, it does," she stated, piqued by his apparent unconcern. "Curt, I know you must have had a reason to kill—"

"So I'm guilty until proven innocent, right?"

His quiet words stung her. Truthfully, she had already tried and convicted him, without the benefit of judge and jury. The police had a digital tape of the crime; she'd as good as seen him do it. And then there was the damning evidence of the gun. How could he have gotten Salty's gun if he hadn't—

"We're here," he stated, interrupting her jumbled thoughts as they reached her Jeep. "Get out your keys."

Having little choice, she fished her keys out of her purse and placed them in his waiting hand. He closed his fingers around them like a vise, then bent to unlock and open her car door.

"Get in," he commanded.

She looked at the open door, knowing that this might be the last chance for her to save herself—and him. "Curt, it's not too late. You can still turn yourself in. Don't add kidnapping to your crimes—"

"Why not? What's a little kidnapping compared to murder? In fact, what's another murder? I can only die once." With unholy calm he leveled the gun at her stomach, then nodded toward the car door. "Now get in. And don't make me ask you a third time, Angel. I'd hate to have to kill a" he paused, his mouth curving up in a humorless smile as he added—"an old friend."

". . . at the Kimbell Museum in downtown Fort Worth. Police emphasize that Mr. Brennermen is only wanted for questioning in the murder, but at this point he is their only suspect—"

Swearing, Curt switched off the car radio. It hadn't taken the media vultures an hour to sniff out his scent. But then, it never did.

He was a hunter by nature. Whether it was cattle or crude oil, he was always the one who pursued, who controlled, and who ultimately conquered. Now a twist of fate had reversed his role, and for the first time in his life he was the prey. And he hated it with all the passion and fury in his predator's soul.

He shifted against the back of the driver's seat, trying to find a comfortable position. No such luck. He was stiff with cold, and his head still ached like crazy. Frustrated, he looked at the speedometer and discovered he was going well over the highway speed limit. Too fast. Might alert cops. *Think like the hunted, not the hunter.*

A muffled cough from the seat beside him reminded him that in one respect at least, he was still the hunter. The thought gave him no pleasure. He glanced at his hostage. She looked too pale, and as fragile as blown glass. His heart twisted at the sight. She didn't deserve this and God knew he didn't want to use her, but he had no choice. She was his only way out of the tight noose the police had thrown around the museum. And she had information he needed, information that might prove his innocence. *Or nail down the lid on my coffin.*

"Tell me about what you saw on the tape," he said quietly.

"Why? You were there," she shot back.

He grinned, surprisingly relieved that she was still mad as hell at him. "Humor me. Tell me about the tape."

"It's not going to do you any good. You should be talking to your lawyer, not kidnapping me."

"I'll pass for now, thanks," he said grimly. "Celebrity trials drag out for months, even years. I don't intend to spend the next few years of my life in jail—especially in a Texas jail."

"You'd get a fair trial."

"I'd get strung up by my . . . You know how many enemies my father made in this state. And revenge is never out of season."

She opened her mouth to fire back a scathing remark, but apparently thought better of it. She sat back against the seat, a slight but undeniable frown turning down the corners of her lips. Those hot, take-me-to-heaven-and-back lips, he thought. *Don't think about it, Brennermen. You've got problems enough without adding that one.*

"Where are we going, anyway?"

His smile died. Whether she realized it or not, she was already in danger of being charged as an accessory to murder. The less she knew, the better. "That's my business, not yours. Tell me what you saw on the tape. And remember, I know plenty of ways to get what I want out of you. . . ."

His threat did the trick. Haltingly, with pauses for what was obviously a great deal of restrained emotion, she told him about the digital recording. He tried to concentrate on what she was saying, disregarding the tremor in her voice as ruthlessly as he ignored personal feelings in his business dealings. Yet somehow he couldn't seem to separate Lyn's words from her pain, any more than he could separate his heart from its beat.

Seven years ago he'd cut her out of his life

with a surgeon's skill. Now, on a lonely road in the middle of Texas nowhere, he discovered the operation wasn't as successful as he'd thought it was. Her soft voice stirred memories deep inside him—of sweet days and sweeter nights, and of a peace that he'd given up along with the proud, foolish, impossible dreams of his youth. *You did what you had to, Brennermen. Don't look back. Never look back.*

". . . and then you pushed him on the floor, and shot him," she said, her voice dropping to a strained whisper. "How could you, Curt? He was no match for a man like you. You never even gave him a chance."

He tightened his grip on the steering wheel. "I didn't do it, Lyn. We argued, but that's all. When I left the gallery someone knocked me out, and I woke up with the gun in my hand."

"How do you explain the tape?" she asked quietly.

"I can't," he growled, frustrated to the core. "Somebody set me up."

Her silence was more damning than any accusation.

To hell with her, he thought. She didn't believe him, and nothing he said would make her believe him. He raked his hand through his hair, wishing like hell that he hadn't brought her with him. But he needed her car, and he needed her knowledge of the computer system. Her trust was optional.

A wet snow had begun to fall. He switched on the windshield wipers, startled at how loud they sounded in the enforced silence of the front seat. The weather was deteriorating. So was his patience. She thought he was guilty. All right, he'd use that to his advantage. He reached down and rested his hand on the handle of the automatic in his waistband, ignoring her quiet gasp of fear. *Never look back.* "Tell me what else the police asked you," he commanded. "And in case you're thinking about extending the silent treatment, darlin', remember, I've still got the gun."

FIVE

The weather grew worse. The temperature dropped, freezing the snow on the road into sheets of black, treacherous ice. Snow continued to fall, blowing in twisting snakes of white across the slick, icy surface. Outside the Jeep, the wind howled like a lost, damned soul. Inside, Lyn placed her palm flat against the ice-cold pane of the passenger window and stared out into the swirling darkness, trying to make sense of her own swirling emotions.

She glanced at the man beside her, at his shadowed features and unforgiving frown. Silence wrapped him like a cloak, distancing him far more than the few feet of space between them. He seemed carved of granite. Mount Rushmore could have taken lessons.

It had been over a half hour since he'd finished asking her questions, and he hadn't spoken since. At first she'd been grateful, but as the minutes ticked by she found herself growing more and more uncomfortable. He was a murderer, a kidnapper, and Lord only knew what else, but as she studied the rugged profile of the stranger who wasn't a stranger at all, the doubts began to creep in. Could a man change that much in seven years? Could the man she'd once loved become a murderer?

"See anything you like?" he asked suddenly.

"Not much," she replied tartly, unwilling to let him guess the direction of her thoughts.

He gave a short laugh, the first unguarded sound he'd made all evening. "You never did have much sympathy for my ego, did you? Even on that summer night when I brought your brother home. Remember?"

How could I forget? She had just completed her sophomore year of college and was spending the summer at Corners, her adopted family's east Texas ranch, where she was taking extra courses at the local community college.

One evening, while her parents were away on a cattle-buying trip, Curt Brennermen had shown up at the door with her younger brother, Rafe, in tow—her very drunk younger brother. On a dare, Rafe had crashed a keg party, and had downed at least four tall-boy cans of beer by the time Curt spotted the underage drinker and hauled his sorry soul on home.

Curt had rescued her brother, but Lyn hadn't known that. The man had a reputation for trouble that stretched back to his high-school days, when she'd been a shy, introverted junior and he'd been a wild, hell-raising senior. And according to the county gossips, he'd grown far worse in the three years since that time. Some even hinted that if his last name hadn't been Brennermen, he'd have been cooling his heels in the county jail.

When Lyn saw Curt with her inebriated brother, she'd immediately jumped to the wrong conclusion. She assumed Brennermen's devil son purposely led the wayward boy astray. And she'd told him exactly what she thought of him—in precise, colorful detail. "Well, maybe I was a little hard on you."

"A little?" he said in mock disbelief. "You practically chewed my head off. You used words even *I* didn't know."

"My misspent youth," she said, falling into the memory. She didn't know which of them had been more shocked: she herself, because Brennermen's scoundrel son turned out to have a heart of gold; or him, because the Tyrell's prim daughter could swear like a sailor.

"That was the first night I called you Angel."

"The moves you tried on me were anything but angelic," she fired back, feeling suddenly uncomfortable.

"Yeah, but you agreed to go out with me anyway," he said as he stared at the road ahead, his mouth curved in a surprisingly wistful smile. "You *were* my angel that summer. The best part of me . . ."

His voice was like a caress. She swallowed, held hostage by the unexpected tenderness of his smile, and the memory of the moment when they'd first gazed into each other's eyes. They'd looked beneath the masks the world made them wear and discovered they were kindred spirits. In that moment a cautious, wholly unexpected friendship sprang up between the county's worst rounder and its purest sweetheart. No one had believed it—no one but the two of them. That was all the belief they'd needed.

Suddenly he cleared his throat, his smile disintegrating back into his usual stern expression. "So," he asked brusquely, "how'd you get mixed up in computers?"

Business as usual, she thought, feeling a sharp, unexpected, and totally inappropriate sense of loss. "I was always good in math, but I didn't want to get stuck in a bank vault all my life. I took a few computer courses and discovered I had a talent for designing them."

"You were always good at fixing broken things," he said in a whisper as soft as the wind.

She didn't know how to take that. She didn't know how to take a lot of things where he was concerned. She wished she'd had more experience with men, but her involvements had been limited at best. And even the most passionate of kisses certainly didn't do one-tenth of the crazy things to her body that just sitting next to Curt did. One-hundredth. "I . . . I worked at Electronic Data Systems for a while," she said, squirming uncomfortably in her seat. "Then about three years ago I joined Guardian, as Salty's—"

Her voice faltered. *Salty.* She looked at her lap and bit her lip, fighting back the sudden sting of tears. She blinked, determined not to cry. But damn, she was going to miss him. . . .

Suddenly she felt the weight of a large, comforting hand on her shoulder. "I know you miss him. It's okay to cry."

The quiet strength of his words released her. She let out a deep ragged sigh—and stopped in abrupt horror when she realized what she was doing. The man comforting her was no friend—he was Salty's murderer! She felt dirty, sickened by his foul, hypocritical comfort. And her eagerness to accept it.

"Don't touch me," she spat, shaking off his arm like it was a viper. She turned back to the passenger window, forcing herself to look out at the dark, bleak winter night. This wasn't the balmy Texas summer of her memory, any more than the man beside her was the rough-edged Romeo she'd loved in the past. She had to remember he was the man who'd callously broken her heart seven years ago. She had to remember he was the man who'd killed her friend and kidnapped her at gunpoint.

She closed her eyes and leaned her burning forehead against the icy pane, confused and more than a little disgusted by her lack of certainty. Curt was a murderer. That was the reality, not some golden dream she'd given up believing in long ago. She had to listen to her head, not her heart—

"Damn," he said suddenly.

She looked back toward him, and saw the reason for his unexpected curse. The low-fuel light had come on. That afternoon she'd bypassed the gas station because she was running late for the gala. Her tardiness may have just saved her skin.

They were going to have to stop for gas. And stopping meant the possibility of escape.

"Are we close to where we're going?" she asked, trying to keep the rising hope out of her voice.

"Not close enough," he admitted sourly. He gripped the wheel and steered the car toward a small side road. "There's an all-night gas station near here. But I want your word that you won't try anything. I want the chance to tell you my side of the story."

"All right," she replied, knowing full well she meant to break her word as soon as she got the chance. She'd already seen his side of the story—at least the part that mattered—on the digital tape. She'd seen the evidence with her own eyes.

Seeing was believing. She'd learned that lesson long ago, during the months she'd spent on the street after she'd run away from home. She'd survived by relying on her five senses, on trusting a person's actions rather than his or her words. That simple truth had saved her neck more than once. If she was lucky and kept her wits about her, it might just save her again.

The time and place had changed, but she was once again fighting for survival. And, once again, she needed to remember to trust in what people did, not what they said. Dr. Osbourne had pointed out that she had a problem trusting people—this time she might be able to use that failing to her advantage. She'd seen more than enough to convince her that Curt was a criminal. He'd run from the police. He'd kidnapped her at gunpoint. He'd killed Salty.

And she hadn't any proof at all that he wouldn't eventually do the same thing to her.

"You have to what?" Curt barked.

Lyn gave him a look as coolly prim as any schoolmarm. "Do I have to repeat it?"

Hell no. He glanced back at the gas-station attendant, who was still in the process of filling the tank, a well-bundled fifty-something man who'd given Curt's tuxedo at least one curious look. He doubted whether news of Salty's murder had made it to this remote part of Texas yet, but when it did he had a bad feeling this guy would remember him.

He shook his head, thinking that hostages were a lot more trouble than those old-time gangster movies made them out to be. "Sorry, Angel. It'll have to wait."

She said nothing.

Damn, he thought as he looked at the forlorn figure huddled in the seat beside him. The woman could do more damage with her silence than an army of Uzi-toting terrorists. But truthfully, his conscience was the real enemy. In the last few hours he'd turned her life inside out—now he was even denying her the most basic of needs. He ran his hand over his face, wishing, not for the first time, that he really was the ruthless murderer she believed him to be. "All right," he bit out. "But I want you to follow my instructions exactly. Or else—" He paused and glanced around, his gaze fixing meaningfully on the attendant. "Or else you might not be the only one who gets hurt."

He got her out of the car and walked her toward the office, making sure that he kept her out of earshot of the station attendant. It wasn't difficult—the rising wind drowned out every sound but its own bitter howl. Still, he wasted no time in grabbing the passkey from the office desk and propelling Lyn around to the side of the building where the rest rooms were located. He shoved the key into the old lock and grabbed the cold metal knob. The biting chill raced up his arm into his shoulder, making him wonder if he'd ever be warm again. Cursing under his breath, he leaned his weight against the reluctant door, forcing it open.

The rest room was clean, but that was possibly the only thing going for it. The brown tile walls were chipped and scored from age, and the linoleum floor was so stained with wear that it was impossible to guess its original color. A single bulb barely illuminated the small space, though the frosted half window in the upper corner probably let in a measure of light during the day. It was almost as cold inside the rest room as it was outside. Curt turned to Lyn and gave her a wry smile. "Not exactly your kind of place, is it?"

"On the contrary, it's just what I need," she

replied as she glanced around the room. She reached for the key, but he held it out of her grasp.

"I'll hold on to this."

"But I won't be able to lock the door."

"That's right," he agreed, his smile fading. "You won't."

She stared at him as if he'd stripped her of her last shred of dignity. Maybe he had. Nevertheless, she raised her chin and marched past him with the composure of a queen. "At least knock before you come in. Surely even an animal like you can do that much," she said, slamming the door behind her.

Animal. The word burned into him like a cattle brand. He told himself it didn't matter, that he didn't give a damn how she felt about him. But as he pulled up his collar against the miserable weather, he had to admit it mattered a great deal.

She'd been the first person who'd ever believed he could make something of himself. Most of the people in the east Texas county he grew up in, including his self-righteous father, had figured he was heading straight to hell. Curt figured he'd end up there, too, until Lyn had looked beyond his tough, defensive exterior and shown him the man he could be. She'd challenged him to learn, offering to tutor him in summer-school courses. She discovered his slight problem with dyslexia, but instead of calling him lazy or stupid, as others had done, she'd worked with him to improve his reading skills, without judgment or censure.

He'd never understand why she'd taken the trouble with him. He was no prize in those days—an irresponsible young buck who had a reputation for drinking, fighting, swearing, and womanizing that was unmatched in the county. Any other sensible woman would have run for the hills. But not Lyn. She'd taught him to look at his strengths rather than his weaknesses. She'd helped him to discover his talents, which unexpectedly included a horse trader's innate understanding of the business of making money. She'd been a friend to him when he'd most needed one. And when he'd needed her to be more than a friend, she'd been that too. . . .

A faint, oddly musical sound jarred his thoughts, but he ignored it. It was probably just the wind—a wind that still wasn't cold enough to cool his hot blood. *Damn!* Why were the memories still so strong? It was crazy to feel this way about a woman who hadn't been a part of his life for seven years—whom he'd purposely cut out of his life. A woman who despised him so much that she cringed in disgust from even his most innocent overtures of companionable comfort. *Never look back.*

Stifling something dangerously like regret, he turned his mind to his other worries. There were plenty to choose from. A man was dead, and everyone and their brother thought he was responsible. The police even had a tape of him killing Saltsgaver. The evidence against him was so damning that if it weren't for the aching bruise on the back of his head, Curt himself might have wondered if he hadn't committed the crime.

But he knew better. The bottom line was that someone had killed an innocent man and had set Curt up to take the fall. That made coming up with the identity of the real killer doubly important. The police had "proof" that he'd done it—and he doubted that they'd waste their time or the taxpayers' money looking for someone else. It was up to Curt to find Salty's killer, though as of this moment he hadn't a clue who that might be.

Except that he has one hell of a swing, he thought as he rubbed the sore spot just above his right ear. He had enemies; he'd learned to play rough during his years in the South American oil fields, and had kept that style even though his circumstances had changed. His take-no-prisoners business style had angered more than a few fat-cat bureaucrats with long arms and longer memories. But he couldn't imagine any of them having the guts to kill a man. Still, *someone* had found the necessary courage, and unless he figured out who that was, he was going to be spending a very long time in a very small cell—

Once again the muffled sound distracted him. He lifted his head and looked around. There was no one nearby, and no possible source for the unusual sound. *Great, now I'm hearing things. Not surprising, considering I'm tired, cold, and have a murder-kidnapping charge hanging over my head. Maybe I'll get a couple months knocked off for letting my hostage have restroom privileges*, he thought with a humorless smile.

That smile died as he heard the sound for a third time and realized that it was coming from the rest room.

He shoved the key into the lock and pushed on the door, only to find it wouldn't budge. Cursing, he rammed his shoulder into the door with all his strength, easily breaking the chair she'd set against the inside knob. The door swung open.

Lyn had wrapped her coat around her fist and broken the glass in the high windowpane. Now she was struggling to pull herself through the empty pane, despite the razor-sharp shards that still framed the small opening.

Christ, she was going to be cut to ribbons! He grasped her waist and yanked her back down, seating her with a thump on the yellowed Formica countertop. He pulled open her fingers and ran his hands along her arms and neck, searching for glass cuts. Her dress was ripped in several places, but he couldn't find any trace of blood. He breathed a short, silent prayer of relief. A person could die within minutes from a severed artery. He'd seen it happen.

"Lyn, are you nuts? You could have killed yourself."

"And saved you the trouble."

He looked up from her hands and saw the naked terror in her eyes. *Idiot, of course she thinks you're going to kill her. She thinks you're a murderer. You've let her think you're a murderer.*

He closed his eyes, feeling a stab of guilt that made his pounding headache seem like nothing. "Lyn," he said roughly, folding her small hands in his. "This whole night has been crazy. But you've got to believe I'd never do anything to hurt—"

The rest-room door opened, and the station attendant walked in. He glanced at the shattered glass, then at the couple by the sink. His eyes narrowed in profound suspicion. "What in the Sam Hill is going on here?"

Hope flared in Lyn's eyes. Curt knew that her terror had made her reckless, and that she was going to tell the attendant everything unless he stopped her. His gun was shoved deep in his cummerbund—he couldn't retrieve it be-

fore she cried a warning and alerted the man.
There was no time to consider consequences,
no time to do anything but react. He wrapped
his fingers around the back of her neck and
pulled her roughly to him, covering her confession with a mouth-consuming kiss.

SIX

Lyn struggled in his arms, trying to pull away. No use. His hold on her neck was like iron, forcing her closed lips against his with a passionless but muffling kiss. Any sound she made would be effectively silenced.

"Dammit, I didn't do it," he murmured against her mouth.

She shivered, her resolve fighting with her compassion. What if he didn't do it? she thought. She recalled her previous doubts, but shoved them forcefully away. Whatever she felt, this was war, and he was the enemy. It was her duty to turn him in.

Drawing back her knee, she landed a decisive kick on his upper thigh. It wasn't exactly the placement she'd hoped for, but it was enough to startle him. For a split second his hold relaxed and she twisted away, freeing half her mouth. Over Curt's shoulder she caught sight of the confused-looking attendant in the rest-room doorway. "Please," she said, trying to make her words intelligible. "Please, he—"

She got no further. Once again Curt's mouth took hers, this time with bruising force. There was no time for her to close her lips, no time to prevent the erotic jolt that came from joining her open mouth to his. It wasn't something either of them had planned, but suddenly she was filled with the taste of him, the heat of his breath, the sensual explosion of his tongue meeting hers. She felt his rough, impossibly gentle fingers loosen the tight bun at the nape of her neck, unraveling her hair as easily as his kiss unraveled her senses.

She reeled inwardly, feeling as if she'd been hit by a freight train. She wasn't supposed to feel like this, like every nerve ending in her body had suddenly become a sizzling fuse. She wasn't supposed to want this. She wasn't supposed to want him.

If he is innocent . . .

Once again she tried to cry out, but the words sounded more like a moan than a protest. Small wonder when he was massaging the back of her neck, turning her spine to Jell-O. Memories burned through her, fueling fires in places she'd forgotten she had.

Years had passed, but he remembered exactly how and where she liked to be touched.

Just as she remembered exactly how and where he liked it. She lifted her fists, intending to beat them against him. Instead, her traitorous hands snaked around his torso, exploring the rock-solid muscles underneath his silk shirt. Touching him was like a drug, tasting him was heaven. It was wrong to react this way, all wrong.

But it felt so damn *right*.

"Lyn," he whispered against her cheek. "Help me."

His plea broke her heart. She'd seen enough innocent people accused and sent to prison to know it could happen to anyone. She also knew that confining a man like Curt to a cell would be the next best thing to a death sentence. She shivered, realizing more than ever that she held his future in her hands. *If he is innocent* . . .

Her hand brushed the hard shape of the gun stuck beneath his waistband.

Fragile towers of hope she didn't even know she was building crumbled into ruin. The gun made a liar out of his words, his need, his kiss. She wanted to scream her anger at the bastard, but she didn't dare. Too clearly she remembered the threats he'd made against the attendant. She was furious enough to risk her own safety, but she couldn't jeopardize some-one else's.

"That's enough!" exclaimed the irate attendant. "I don't know what kinky things you two perverts are into, but you're not gonna do 'em in *my* station."

Curt stiffened, his expression unreadable. He reached under his jacket, and for a sickening moment Lyn thought he was going to pull out the gun. Instead, he took out his wallet and stuffed a sizable amount of bills into the surprised attendant's outstretched palm. "That should cover the gas and the window," he stated. Then he took Lyn's hand and led her out into the night.

The wind had picked up, whipping the strands of her unbound hair against her cheeks. The temperature had dropped to well below freezing, but even the change in degrees couldn't touch the chill in Lyn's heart. She glanced at the dark, silent figure walking beside her, then back toward the lighted office of the station, thinking how tantalizingly close she'd come to freedom. Might-have-beens filled her mind. If only she'd managed to escape through the window. If only she'd had the presence of mind to slip a note to the attendant. If only Curt hadn't kissed her. How could something so wrong feel so damn r—

"Thank you."

His rough baritone ignited a number of feelings inside her, none of them welcome. "I didn't do it for you," she fired back. "I was afraid you'd shoot that attendant—like you shot Salty."

"You still think I did it." He sighed.

She looked away, hating how aware she was of the disappointment in his voice. It was a lie, it had to be. "I *know* you did it. And don't think you can seduce me into believing differently."

His shadowed expression didn't waver, but his iron fingers tightened around her wrist. "Don't worry, I never make the same mistake twice," he promised with lethal softness. "Remember that the next time you think about escaping."

Three A.M. Curt read the digital display on the Jeep's dashboard, then rubbed his tired eyes. He'd been up since seven that morning, but that had been Bahamas time, which put it an hour or two earlier. Maybe three. He grimaced, recalling the days when he'd stayed up for forty-eight hours at a stretch on the South American drilling sites, fighting fatigue, poor equipment, and undisciplined workers to finish the job before torrential rains turned his hard work into a muddy puddle. Only a handful of years had passed since those early adventures, but he felt as if he'd aged a lifetime. I'm getting too old for this, he thought.

He glanced at the woman curled against the passenger door, and felt something like a miniature depth charge explode in his abdomen. *Way too old.*

There had been other women in his life. He made no apologies—he was a healthy, red-blooded man with a healthy, red-blooded appetite for passion, and he enjoyed the sensual pleasures of love as much as his partners. During the early years in the jungles of South America, he'd worked hard and played hard, using sex as release from a dangerous, back-breaking job that could have gotten him killed at any minute.

Two years ago the wells had come in and his fortunes had abruptly changed, but he'd still avoided lasting commitments. He'd told himself his constant travel made relationships impossible, and that it had nothing to do with what he'd had with Lyn. How could it? They'd spent a summer together, that's all. She was a memory, a sweet, almost forgotten memory.

That's what he'd told himself . . . until her kiss proved him the biggest liar ever born.

It wasn't a memory he'd held in his arms— it was a living, breathing woman whose tenderness set him on fire. It was the wrong time, the wrong place, and—from her point of view—the wrong man. But that hadn't stopped the magic from happening between them again. And it hadn't stopped the killing emptiness in his soul when she'd told him she was only doing it to save that blasted attendant's skin.

Never look back.

Grimacing, he turned his eyes to the lane ahead, one of the winding farm-to-market roads that crisscrossed Texas like a drunken grid. Live oak and cedars banked right up to the edge of the lane, their barren branches encased in layers of glittering ice. The Jeep's headlights caught an ancient signpost lying by the side of the road, toppled over by the storm. I'll have to fix that next summer, he thought. Providing he was still around next summer.

"We're almost there," he said aloud.

"Where?"

"My vacation house," he explained, ignoring her less-than-enthusiastic tone. "I built it a year ago and buried its ownership through so many shell corporations, it'd take a law class to dig it out. There are no phones, no television, no distractions, and best of all, no press." He shook his head, thinking again how crazy things had gotten. "I never thought I'd be using it as a hideout."

She looked down and smoothed a crease in her creaseless knit skirt. In the same, dull tone, she asked, "What happens now?"

Well, at least she's talking. "Good things. Great things. A hot shower, a solid meal, and a long sleep on a soft—"

"No," she interrupted, her voice heavy with strain. "I meant, what happens to me?"

It was a good question. Unfortunately, he

didn't have a good answer. He hadn't exactly planned ahead when he'd commandeered her Jeep to make his escape. Oh, he'd considered a few scenarios, but all of them depended on her believing in his innocence. He'd counted on her help and her trust. He gripped the wheel, realizing too late that he'd let himself begin to count on other things too—things that didn't have a chance in hell of happening.

"I'm making this up as I go along," he confessed. "But it'd be nice if, just for a minute, you'd at least consider the possibility that I might be innocent."

He braced himself for a caustic reply. Instead she sat up and pushed aside her pale fall of hair, staring at him speculatively. He winced, bracing himself for a completely different reaction. He had pulled her hair out of its sophisticated bun and her dress was in tatters, but she was still the most beautiful woman he'd ever seen. *Bad timing, Curt. Real bad timing*.

She spoke, her words as cautious and measured as her gaze. "If you didn't kill Salty, then who did?"

It wasn't much, but it was a start, and he seized on it like a hungry hawk on a mouse. "I only saw a shadow. One minute I was in the gallery talking with Salty—"

"You said you were *arguing* earlier," she said with a sharp glance.

Nothing gets by her, even when she's scared out of her wits, he thought with grudging admiration. "I guess you'd call it arguing. Saltsgaver told me he thought someone was embezzling from Guardian, but he wouldn't tell me who. Said he wanted more proof before he gave me the name of the sidewinder who—why are you looking like that?"

"That's what he told me," she said slowly, as if remembering. "He said he'd just heard something from a sidewinder. I thought he meant you."

"If the rattle fits . . . Anyway, I started to leave the gallery. The next thing I knew I was waking up next to a dead body with a gun in my hand and a lump the size of North Dakota on the back of my head."

"Where did you get hit?" she asked quietly.

"Here," he said, pointing to a spot behind his right ear. "It still aches like craz—"

His words ended abruptly as she reached out and gently brushed her fingers over the spot he'd indicated. Her touch was feather-light, but he winced from even the slight pressure on the tender spot. Still, it was worth it. Her caring touch may not have done much for the knot on his head, but it soothed his soul in a way that defied description.

Since this nerve-racking night began he'd been lost in a maze without exits, but her touch gave him hope that there might be a way out.

Believe me, Angel. I need someone to believe in me.
"Checking out my story?"

She drew back her hand, clearly uncertain.
"I used to help my brother Micah with his
premed exams. I know about concussions. A
blow in that area can be—"

"Fatal. I know. I used to do the doctoring
on the jungle well sites." He glanced at the
woman beside him, studying her as closely as
she'd studied him. "Now do you believe me?"

"I don't know," she said honestly. "You
could have fallen. Or Salty could have hit you
during your fight."

"You know as well as I do that a fist doesn't
make this kind of dent in a man's skull. And I
didn't fight with him, no matter what you saw
on the tape. We argued, but that's all. The tape
is a fake."

She shook her head. "Impossible. I know
that computer equipment. I helped design it. It
was created with strict security protocol guide-
lines. The camera doesn't lie."

"And I do?"

She looked away, her delicate profile edged
by the faint light from the dashboard. "You did
before," she said softly.

It was an old accusation—six years old—but
it cut through him with the pain of a newly
sharpened blade. "I had a new life in South
America, a life you couldn't be a part of."

"You don't have to repeat it. I read your

letter saying you'd gotten used to your freedom, and you weren't coming back to Texas . . . or me."

"Okay, I lied when I left Texas," he stated, his patience stretched to the breaking point by fatigue and frustration. "My dad had just died, for crissake. I was twenty-one and restless and scared stiff I was going to grow old and die in east Texas nowhere."

"*I* was part of that east Texas nowhere!"

"Yeah, you were," he agreed roughly. "And maybe I was just a little afraid of you too."

She opened her mouth, but shut it again without replying. At least I've put a dent in her thick skull too, he thought as he passed the wooden gate and pulled into the driveway of his house. If she questioned the past, she might be more willing to question the present.

We've come to the wrong house, Lyn thought as she walked toward the door of Curt's home. The nor'wester's frigid drizzle had ceased for the moment and Curt had already switched on the front lights from the garage, allowing her to take a good look at the two-story building. She'd expected something out of *Lifestyles of the Rich and Famous*—expensive, showy, and huge. But this unpainted frame structure nestled among the live oaks and cedars was almost, well, charming.

Brass coach lamps framed the glass-paned front door, illuminating the thick tangle of honeysuckle vines that surrounded the first floor. They were coated with a glaze of ice now, but in the spring and summer they would bloom with a thousand fragrant blossoms.

The inside was just as unexpected. The ceiling was two stories high, and reinforced by thick beams of rough-hewn oak. The left wall was a large, natural stone fireplace, while the right was entirely covered by light pine bookshelves. The wall she faced was entirely glass, and though she could only imagine what scene lay beyond the night-dark window, she suspected it would be spectacular.

A gallery with a wood railing encircled the second story on three sides, with doors leading off to what she assumed were upstairs bedrooms. An island bar completed the room, separating the spacious living area from a modern kitchen.

It was a striking room, but it was also well designed and functional. The leather furniture was decidedly masculine, and the hardwood floors were covered by the traditional geometric symmetry of Navaho rugs. There was even a pair of antlers mounted over the fireplace. It was definitely a man's domain and she skimmed her hand along the soft back of the leather couch, fascinated in spite of herself by the unrepentantly male character of the room.

Her own tastefully decorated apartment in Dallas seemed cluttered and lifeless by comparison.

She heard a heavy scrape behind her. Turning, she saw Curt elbowing open the front door, his arms loaded down with wood. "Thought we could use this," he commented as he headed for the fireplace. "The temperature's still dropping out there."

Lyn was only half listening. She looked at the open door and the freedom beyond. If she ran out into the woods, chances were that he wouldn't be able to find her in the dark. She could make a break for it—

"I wouldn't try it if I were you," he said, reading her mind. "The nearest house is miles away. You'd freeze before you found it. *If* you found it. Face it—you're stuck here." He dropped the wood, hunkered down in front of the fireplace, and began to lay the cedar logs in the grate. "Might as well make the best of it."

She didn't want him to be right—trading the house for the car seemed little better than exchanging one prison for another. No matter how agreeable the surroundings, she was still his hostage, and he was still her captor. The only thing she could do was bide her time, and look for an opportunity to escape.

She closed the front door and walked back, settling herself in one of the large side chairs that flanked the fireplace. The supple leather molded to her form, drawing the tension from her too taut limbs. The fatigue she'd kept at bay for hours began to fall around her like a thick, comforting cloak. She pulled her legs up under her and leaned her cheek against the chair's side, watching Curt as he built the fire.

There was an easy, unhurried grace to the way he laid the wood on the grate. He studied each log as if it had a particular character, and set it on the fire as carefully as an accomplished artist places paint on a canvas. When he was done he took a long match from the brass cylinder on the fireplace mantel and struck it against the stone hearth, then set it to the logs.

It took less than a minute for the dry wood to catch into a cheerful, crackling blaze. Almost instantly the smell of burning cedar filled the room, tickling Lyn's nose with its sharp, spicy scent. She snuggled deeper into the chair, letting the warmth of the fire seep into her cold and tired body. I'm not falling asleep, she assured herself. I'm just resting my eyes.

To prove it, she opened her eyes again and caught sight of Curt standing in front of the fireplace with his strong hands gripping the stone mantel, his head bent in concentration. He'd taken off his tuxedo jacket and had rolled his shirtsleeves up to the elbows, exposing the corded muscles of his arms. The firelight licked across his bronze skin, accenting the strength of his form, the hands that could be so cruelly harsh, or so achingly tender. Emotions battled within her.

His story about arguing with Salty was plausible, especially with what her boss had told her in the hallway leading to the gallery. But Salty wasn't necessarily talking about an embezzler—he could have been irritated with any of the party guests, for any reason. Curt's explanation was flimsy at best, and she only had his word for it. The word of a fugitive, a kidnapper, a possible murderer . . . and someone she'd once been deeply in love with. Her eyes drifted shut, her weary mind reeling from the unwieldy combination.

"The police are going to find us eventually," she stated.

His low, humorless chuckle rumbled through her like thunder. "Spoken like a proper hostage. But don't get your hopes up. The only one who knows about this place is Benny, and he won't talk."

"How can you be so sure?"

"Because he's my friend," he said, more to himself than to her. "Lord knows I've got few enough of those."

"Hardly surprising."

He flashed her a devilish grin, a ghost of his former self. For an instant she felt the strong, sweet camaraderie that used to bind them together like two halves of the same heart. But the feeling didn't last. He turned back to the fire, his grin deteriorating into a shadowed expression that even the bright flames couldn't warm.

"They say it's lonely at the top, but that's not true. It's crowded as hell. Everywhere I look, there are people who want something from me—who see me for what I have rather than what I am. They swarm around me like bloodsucking mosquitoes, fawning and grasping, pretending undying friendship when you know they wouldn't give me the time of day a few years ago." He bent his head, as if the weight of the world rested on his shoulders. "I've learned to appreciate my true friends, Lyn."

She bit her lip, feeling his heartsickness as if it were her own. As ambiguous as her feelings were for Curt, she hated to think of him surrounded by lesser men, and opportunistic women. He was strong, but in time, people like that would drain him dry. It was ridiculous considering her circumstances, but she suddenly felt like he was the one who needed protecting.

"I'm tired, Lyn," he confessed in words as old as time. "In body and in soul. I don't want to argue anymore. I don't want to think. Can't we call a truce, just for tonight?"

His dark eyes caught the light of the flickering fire. She felt the strength in him, the power that set him apart from other men, but she also sensed his vulnerability, and the risk he'd taken in showing it to her. Only a strong man would do that. Only a confident man. Only an innocent man . . .

Or a man who was guilty and trying to convince her he wasn't.

Curt had said he valued his friends. Well, she did, too, and Salty had been one of them. She couldn't just discount the evidence of the police tape because of some . . . feeling. She had rotten instincts when it came to Curt Brennermen. The thanks-for-the-memories letter he'd sent her from South America was proof of that.

Six years ago he'd dumped her without looking back, but she was older now and, she hoped, wiser. She intended to judge him by empirical evidence, not by fickle, undependable emotions. And the empirical evidence was about as damning as it came.

He'd kidnapped her. He'd stolen her car to escape the police. There was the tape—the tape that sealed his guilt as unequivocally as any confession. "You know, if you give yourself up, they might not—"

"Christ, didn't you hear anything I said?" he cried as he left the fire and strode toward her.

He stopped in front of her and bent down, gripping the arms of the chair. His face was in shadow, but she could still feel the fire burning in his eyes—burning into hers. His nearness unnerved her. His passion energized her. Her entire body kicked into high gear when he was near, and right now he was a whole lot nearer than she wanted him to be.

She pressed her back flush against the leather upholstery, putting every inch of distance she could between them. "Please," she said without really knowing what she was asking. "Please, I—"

"I've known some hard-hearted characters in my time, but you top them all. I'd like nothing better than to kick your judgmental little hide out in the storm and good riddance, but I need your technical knowledge to figure out who doctored that tape."

"It can't be doctored," she said, finding it unaccountably hard to breathe. "I already told you that."

"Find a better answer," he ordered, leaning so close she could feel the heat of his breath. "I want your cooperation. And I'm not real choosy about how I get it."

SEVEN

The fire had burned down to glowing embers. Curt stood with his foot propped on the hearth, watching the flames die. He picked up the brass poker, intending to use it to coax a final blaze from the ashes, but decided against it. Some fires shouldn't be stirred back to life, he thought as he replaced the poker. Some fires, and some passions . . .

He glanced over toward the chair that held Lyn's silent, shadow-wrapped figure. "We need some sleep."

"I'm not sleepy," she replied, though she had to stifle a yawn to say it.

His smile deepened. Exhausted, scared, and pushed to the limit, she still hadn't lost her courage. *Good thing I'm running on empty myself. Otherwise sleep wouldn't be the only thing on my mind.* "We both need some sleep, Angel. You can walk upstairs or I can carry you. Your choice."

"Some choice," she grumbled, but that was the only protest she made. Truthfully, the thought of a bed and a few hours of undisturbed slumber sounded absolutely wonderful. Guiltily, she knew she should put up more of a fight for Salty's sake, but she was just too damn tired. *I need a couple hours of rest, and I don't care where,* she thought pragmatically as she climbed the stairs. *He can lock me in a closet with a mattress for all I care.*

But the room he led her to wasn't a closet —it was the master bedroom. Large and spacious, it was decorated in the same southwestern style as the living room. A huge antique wardrobe and an old rolltop desk took up one wall, while a bank of electronic equipment and a door to a private bathroom occupied the opposite side. In between was a king-size brass bed with a thick down comforter the color of the sunset.

Lyn walked over and sat heavily on the bed. It felt like pure heaven. Exhausted, she buried her face in her hands, asking God, Salty, and whoever else happened to be listening to forgive her for not putting up more of a fight. *I promise I'll be tough and tenacious again tomorrow, but right now I just want to sleep—*

She heard the door close. Raising her head, she frowned as she saw Curt still standing on her side of the door. "I'm sorry, but I'm just not up for any more questions tonight. You'll have to wait until tomorrow."

"Suits me fine," he said as he opened the door to the wardrobe.

Shouldn't he be leaving around now? "I suppose the sooner we get to sleep, the sooner we can get up."

"Sounds like a plan," he agreed with a nonchalant shrug. He rolled down his sleeves and began to unbutton his dress shirt.

Apparently he wasn't taking the hint. "Curt, I'd like to get some sleep, so I'd appreciate it if you'd le—"

Her words died as he stripped off his shirt, revealing a broad, tanned back of wall-to-wall muscles. Oh God, she thought, feeling her courage fade as her temperature rose. He was even more beautiful than she remembered. His early strength had matured into a clean, sleek power that seemed to radiate from him like light from the sun. *I can't remember what we were to one another. I'll go crazy.* "I really think you should leave now."

"Too bad," he commented as he hung up his shirt and closed the door on the wardrobe. "Which side of the bed do you want?"

"Which *side*?" she said in horror as she rose from the bed. "My Lord, you can't seriously believe . . . I mean, you don't think I'm going to *sleep* with you."

"That's the general idea," he commented as he closed the wardrobe door.

He's not kidding, she thought, her panic increasing with each passing second. She turned and bolted for the door, but the knob wouldn't budge. She was locked in. With him.

She leaned her head against the door and rattled the ineffectual knob, fighting tears of anger, exhaustion, and terror. "I knew you were despicable, but I never thought you'd—"

A strong hand covered her own. "Jesus, don't you ever get tired of believing the worst of me?"

"Never," she cried, using anger to fuel her fearlessness. It was sham courage at best. She was far too aware of the heat of his half-naked body, and far too aware of her own body's re-action to him. *I shouldn't feel this way. I can't feel this way.* "You're a murderer and a kidnapper, and now you're a rap—"

"The hell I am," he growled, spinning her around. He gripped her shoulders and stared down at her, his dark eyes burning into hers with a demon light. "When I said sleep I meant *sleep*. I'm too damn tired for anything else. But even if I weren't, I'd sooner take a block of ice to bed than you. Less of a chal-lenge."

He released her so quickly, she almost stumbled. He gave her a last, chilling stare, then turned to the bed and yanked down the covers. "I'll take the left side," he muttered as he switched out the light. "You can take the right side or the floor—you'll be just as safe in either place, trust me. And don't even think about trying to steal the keys from my pocket. Unless," he added with a smile so wicked it gleamed in the darkness, "you want your foul-minded predictions to come true."

I loathe him, she thought as she stood alone in the sudden, silent darkness. In a few short hours he'd turned her sane, safe life into a catastrophe of biblical proportions. He was a heartless, soulless criminal who'd killed her friend and was very likely going to kill her. She almost wished he would. Then she wouldn't have to feel the humiliating, aching need that twisted through her whenever he so much as touched her. . . .

She wrapped her arms tightly around her middle, as if physical force could hold her fraying emotional state together. It didn't, of course. The feelings boiled up inside her and burned down her cheeks in tears of pain and confusion.

I can't take this, she thought as she ruthlessly rubbed away her tears. I've tried so hard to pretend I'm brave, but I can't do it anymore. I'm tired. I'm scared. I'm at the end of my emotional rope. And I miss Salty. . . .

"Lyn."

His voice in the darkness was close and intimate. She felt the weight of his hands on her shoulders, but this time his touch was gentle, comforting. She stiffened, shocked as much by his tenderness as his nearness.

"It's all right to cry," he said in a voice as soft as worn leather.

"It's not right," she said weakly. "I think—"

"For once in your life *don't* think," he said, pulling her against him. "Stop hiding your feelings behind that icy control of yours. Just cry, Angel. Let it go."

His soothing voice undermined the last of her retraints. She leaned against him and cried out all her fear, heartache, and confusion in huge, messy, soul-raking sobs. It's nuts to be doing this, she thought, especially with him. But she couldn't stop. Tears that had been building in her for what seemed like a lifetime poured out with the violence of the storm outside. She clung to him, drawing on his strength to replace hers, pretending just for a moment that the comfort he offered was real and true, and not a brief act of kindness in a larger, uglier game.

Sometime during her crying spell he got her into bed and tucked the covers up under her chin. She curled up beneath the blankets, feeling small, drained, confused, and a thousand other emotions she was far too tired to name. Sleep wrapped around her like the gossamer strands of a spiderweb, pulling her deeper and deeper into its mind-numbing grasp. "Not right," she muttered as she slipped beyond consciousness. "He killed Salty. Saw it . . ."

Beside the bed, Curt winced at her words. You're an idiot, Brennermen, he thought as he turned away from her. She's never going to believe you. Nothing's changed.

"Curt?"

She wasn't asleep, though the slowness in her speech indicated that she was very close to it. "I'm here."

"Sorry I called you a rapist."

But not that she called him a murderer, he thought bitterly. "Go to sleep, Lyn."

It seemed, for once, she was following his orders. She yawned and burrowed down into the comforter, her breath slowing to an even, steady rhythm. His eyes, now accustomed to the lack of light, picked out the cream paleness of her skin against the darker covers. He watched her, feeling a strange, unfamiliar tenderness creep into his heart.

She sighed in her sleep, yawning like a contented kitten as she breathed, "Gladiators."

Curt's eyes widened in amused surprise. Apparently his once innocent little love now indulged in some very adult fantasies. Somehow, that made her even more endearing. Instinctively he reached out his hand to brush her cheek, but froze as the cruel knife of memory cut through him.

He had no right to touch her. He'd given up that right years ago, when he'd walked away from east Texas, and out of her life.

Back then, his entire life had revolved around loving her. He'd wanted to give her everything she deserved, and with the arrogance of a young man in love, he'd thought that he could. But his fine dreams had crumbled into trail dust. Near the end of their golden summer his father had suffered a sudden, fatal heart attack. As the only son, Curt was suddenly thrust into riding herd on the financial maelstrom of the vast Brennermen empire.

Dealing with Sam Brennermen's sudden death had been hard enough, but dealing with the financial jigsaw puzzle he left behind made it far worse. Curt's younger sister, Cathy, was far too absorbed in playing the grieving daughter to help with anything—except to make certain she got her weekly allowance. Lyn volunteered to help, but Curt wouldn't hear of her putting off her college term for him. Besides, he'd learned enough about finances that summer to suspect that something about his father's practices didn't add up.

The damage turned out to be worse than anyone suspected. Sam Brennermen had lost a considerable amount of money in some risky investments, and had compounded the problem by borrowing to keep up his affluent image. When the dust and creditors cleared, there was nothing left of the Brennermen fortune but a small trust fund left to his sister, Cathy, by their mother, and controlling interest in a speculative oil-drilling operation in South America.

At the time Curt had felt he had no choice but to leave. He needed money to pay the balance of his father's debts, and the wildcat drilling company seemed the only possibility of getting it.

Telling Lyn had been the hardest part. He swore he'd come back to her; at the time he'd even believed it. But the operation proved to be more of a white elephant than a cash cow. He barely broke even, and only accomplished that much by working around the clock for weeks on end.

Exhaustion and disappointment became his constant companions. Lyn's well-meaning letters about her glowing academic career added to his gloom. He'd wanted to give her everything, but as the weeks stretched into months and finally to a year, he admitted to himself that he'd never be able to give her anything more than a mud hole in South America.

He loved her too much to sentence her to that kind of life, so he'd written a letter telling her he'd grown used to his freedom and meant to keep it. How could he have known that four years, eleven months, and fifteen days later one of his misbegotten oil wells would suddenly tap into the richest field known in that part of the world. . . .

"Hell," he muttered into the darkness. The what-ifs could tear a man apart from the inside out if you let them—he'd seen it happen to stronger men than he. After he'd struck it rich he planned to come back for her and even bought a plane ticket, but a good look in the mirror had shown him the truth.

The boy she'd loved was gone, replaced by a hard, stone-faced man, who'd had all his dreams burned out of him. The years of back-breaking labor, of driving himself and the men under him to the edge of exhaustion, of dealing dirty in order to deal with the much dirtier political system, of seeing starving children on every street corner and knowing that the money he gave them would invariably go to their dealer or their pimp . . . those tortured years had left scars on his body and his soul. He was a different man from the reckless dreamer she'd known back in east Texas.

There was nothing left in him for her to love.

"Hell," he cursed again as he rounded the bed to the other side. He was on the run from the law and had a murder rap hanging over his head, but the thing that played over and over again in his mind was the way Lyn had felt in his arms when he'd kissed her. For a moment the years had rolled back, and he was once again the bold, cocksure dreamer she'd fallen in love with. That kiss was almost worth a murder rap, he thought with a reluctant smile. Except, of course, for the fact that when it was over she'd pulled away from him in horror.

There's nothing left in me for her to love.

Outside, the freezing winds rattled the windows, but they were nothing compared with the bitter chill in his own heart. He pulled back the covers, trying his best to ignore the slight figure sleeping on the other side of the bed. No luck. The sound of her soft, measured breathing brought back memories so sweet, they made his chest ache—among other things.

Groaning, he pulled his pillow over his head, hoping to block out the sound. But he couldn't block out the past, the blood memory of what they'd been like together, of a passion so hot it had seared the two of them into one. No other woman had ever made him feel that fire. No other woman had even come close. He was physically drained and emotionally exhausted, but he still craved her with a hunger that reached up from the core of his soul. Just let me fall asleep, he prayed in silent desperation. Just let me fall asleep before I go crazy.

And for once, his prayer was answered.

She was warm, wonderfully warm. All night she'd been having terrible dreams of cold and snow and murder, but now she was surrounded by heat, engulfed by it. Yawning drowsily, she slowly opened her eyes and looked around for the source of the marvelous warmth—and went stone still. A bare masculine arm encircled her waist, a long-fingered male hand lay against her rib cage, just inches below her right breast, and velvet-soft breathing ruffled the hair just behind her ear. Her back was pressed against the solid wall of his chest, and her bottom was cradled in the saddle of his hips. Sometime during the night Curt had pulled her against him in a lovers' intimate embrace—and fallen fast asleep.

Reluctantly, she prepared to pull out of his arms. It was the sensible thing to do, yet she found herself delaying the slight movement that would take her out of his reach. He was asleep, after all. There was no harm in lingering just for a minute. No harm . . .

She liked lying against him, liked the marvelous tingles that radiated from every fiber of her being. She liked feeling the heat and strength of him, of letting her sleep-slowed mind linger over luxurious memories of other mornings long ago. Her sensible nature warned her that she was crazy to do this. *You're playing with fire—pure, undiluted hellfire.*

She didn't listen. Years ago she'd cherished

her wonderful dreams of their future together. They'd been demolished by his rejection, but now—just for a moment and without any risk of him finding out—she could pretend it had all come true.

Gently, gingerly, she let down the wall she kept around herself and unlocked the fragile wishes she'd locked away in her heart. We'd be an old married couple by now, she thought with a soft smile. This morning wouldn't be any different from a hundred others. I'd lie spooned against him until he woke up. And then we'd make slow, unhurried love—

Her thoughts ended abruptly as his arm tightened around her. With a sleepy, contented growl, he shifted his hand and took possession of her breast. She gasped at the unexpected caress, and gasped again at her body's immediate reaction to it. She felt as if she'd been dipped in fire, burning from the inside out. He kneaded her breast to a sweet, aching hardness, until she had to bite her lip to keep from crying aloud at the exquisite torture.

Pull away, her mind warned. Instead, she moved against him, inviting a deeper caress. He was still asleep, she reasoned. And it had been such a long time since she'd been in his arms. . . .

His fingers moved slowly to probe her hardened nipple. She felt his touch through the knit material of her dress, and had to clench her teeth to keep from moaning. He was driving her mad. She knew she should end this, but she'd lost the will. She felt drugged—drugged by the sweet liquid heat of his touch.

He stroked and teased her nipple until she arched uncontrollably against his palm, her body throbbing with unbearable need. He nuzzled the sensitive skin of her neck with his beard-roughened cheek, growling with deep, throaty pleasure. God, he still remembered the spot behind her ear that drove her wild. She wanted his mouth all over her, to have him claim her with his kiss, his touch, his . . .

She swallowed as his other hand wrapped around her and raised her bunched-up skirt, fanning across the bare skin of her stomach. Fireworks exploded inside her. Got to end this, she thought in rising panic. He doesn't know it's me. He's seducing one of his little playmates, not—

"Angel," he murmured hotly against her skin.

The sound of her name shattered her. His need for her—*her*—was the most potent aphrodisiac she'd ever known. She moaned gutterally, consumed by an inferno of memories, dreams, and throbbing, driving need. His skin felt like satin over steel. She pressed back against his naked chest, wrapped by his warmth, his strength, his intoxicating, over-

whelming maleness. God, she needed this . . .
needed him.

For years she'd been alone, as cold and
dead as the dreams that had haunted her sleep.
But his strong, long-fingered hands stroked fire
through her. His rough, nuzzling kisses made
steamy, sizzling desire erupt in her most intimate places. For the first time in years she felt
alive—deliciously, outrageously, sinfully alive.

"Angel," he murmured again, shattering
her anew. She knew he was waking, and the
anticipation almost killed her. He'd pushed
down the back of her panties and pulled her
nakedness against him, so that his half-open
slacks were the only barrier between her and
the hard strength of his arousal. Panting, she
writhed against him, wantonly opening herself
to his bold, stroking caress. *I need him. God,
how I need him.*

She was mad for him. She wanted him like
she wanted her next breath—more. In another
minute he'd wake up, and they'd make sweet,
hot love, just like they used to. . . .

And then what? her conscience questioned.

Who the hell cares? she fired back. She didn't
want to think about the future. She didn't want
to think of anything except the way his long-
fingered hands were kneading her into a
frenzy. Just let me have this, she pleaded silently, desperately. I've been cold and empty

for so long. Just let me have this moment wrapped in his warmth, his life, his love—

And then what?

And then—*nothing*. Once they'd had sex, she'd see their passion for what it was—a cheap, mindless release that would leave her colder and emptier than before. Her fragile dreams came thudding to earth under the harsh weight of reality. This was lust, not love. This was the present, not the past. Dear God, what had she done? He was a fugitive, a kidnapper, and possibly a murderer—but in this instance she was the criminal. She'd done the seducing, not him.

"Curt," she breathed through dry lips, fighting her still-rising passion. "Curt, wake—"

She gasped as his fingers tangled in the hair at the apex of her thighs, claiming her with primitive hunger. Desire lashed her like a whip. She threw back her head, offering her neck to his hot, devouring mouth. It was heaven. It was hell. She wanted him, she *ached* for him—but she couldn't have him.

"Curt, please—" she cried in words torn from her soul. "Please. Wake up."

And this time he did. She heard the sleepy desire in his breath sharpen to a razor hiss of understanding. Quick as thought, he pulled away and backed to the other side of the mattress, the bedsprings groaning under the sudden shift in weight. Lyn felt the groan echo through her own tortured frame. Her body still screamed for him.

She felt him staring at her, heard his harsh breathing as he fought for control. It matched her own. Striving for some semblance of dignity, she sat up and pulled her panties and dress back in place. Her movements were mechanical and slightly ridiculous considering where his hands had been a moment before, but it gave her an excuse not to look at him. She couldn't face him, knowing what she'd almost let him do . . . what she *still* wanted him to do. If he reached for her now, she'd go into his arms without a word, without a regret. Her body burned, but not from shame. How could something so wrong feel so—

His gruff words interrupted her thoughts. "You can use the shower first. I'll dig out some of my sister Cathy's old clothes. They'll probably fit you."

She didn't want to take a shower. He was giving her some time to collect herself—she should be grateful. Yet all she could think about was how much she did *not* want to leave his bed. She'd thought stopping before consummation would make forgetting easier. Instead, it had left her with a soul-deep ache that grew stronger with every heartbeat. Passion alone couldn't have left this mark on her soul.

It was something richer, something truer. Something worth taking risks for.

Her adopted mother had always told her to follow her heart. Nine years ago Sarah Gallegher had taken a chance on a drifter named Luke Tyrell, a man who had a three-state reputation for trouble. The gamble had paid off. Luke had helped Sarah and her adopted children save their home, and Sarah's love had saved Luke from an empty, rootless life. Nine years of marriage had only deepened their love for their children and for one another.

"Trust your heart," Sarah had said. Still, Lyn's mother had never had to wonder if the man she cared for was a murderer. *But I couldn't feel this way about him if he'd murdered Salty. I couldn't.*

Slowly, deliberately, she lifted her gaze to meet his. The morning light filtered through the curtains on the far end of the room, showing his wildly tousled hair and the hair-dusted expanse of his naked torso. His obsidian eyes glittered from beneath stormy brows, yet his mouth was straight, and strangely expressionless, considering what they'd just been through. She could sense the battle raging in him—she could see it in his taut, strained shoulders. Beneath his hard, controlled exterior he was just as uncertain as she was. As uncertain as the proud, stubborn boy she'd once loved . . .

"Curt," she said softly. "Could we talk honestly about—"

His harsh laugh interrupted her. "About what, baby? The fact that we almost . . ."

He used a word so brutal, it made her wince. In a single syllable he destroyed everything that had ever been between them, everything she'd treasured so long in her heart. She'd been wrong about him—horribly, painfully wrong. She backed off the bed, feeling foolish, devastated, cheap. "It won't happen again," she promised coolly as she straightened her shoulders and walked to the bathroom. "Never."

She left without a backward glance. He watched her go in silence, drinking in every move of her body, like a man condemned to hell savors his last glimpse of heaven. And when she was gone he gathered up the sheets she'd slept on, and buried his face in her scent and her warmth.

EIGHT

The room was empty when Lyn got out of her shower. Curt was gone, but he'd left behind the clothes he'd promised on the bed. Cathy's old scoop-necked fishermen's sweater and striped peasant skirt were a size too large and an inch too short for Lyn's tall frame, but she hardly noticed. It was heaven to be out of her bedraggled knit dress; she felt like a new woman. But her feeling of relief was only temporary.

Trying the bedroom door, she found it still locked securely against her. She may have felt like a new woman, but her situation hadn't changed one iota. She was still his prisoner, still in his power. She wrapped her arms around her middle and glanced at the unmade bed, recalling vividly how overwhelming his power could be. But it wasn't just his strength that had kept her in his arms. It was the need that had ached inside her, that still ached inside her. . . .

Wise up! she told herself sternly. Whatever her unreliable emotions told her, Salty was dead—and Curt was the prime suspect in his murder. The police were after him.

She'd seen the digital videotape of him committing the crime. And last night he'd told her that he meant to have her cooperation, and he didn't much care how he got it. She shivered, feeling a little sick inside as she realized that making love to her was one of the easiest ways for him to get her cooperation. God, he'd played her like violin. Or a pennywhistle, considering how eagerly she'd gone into his arms.

But if that was his game, why hadn't he gone through with it?

She had no answers, and every new thought led to more questions. Her mind felt like a Mixmaster on high speed. She rubbed her throbbing temple, certain of one thing and one thing only. She had to escape. She had to get out of this nightmare. She had to get away from him, and back to her safe, sane, empty life, before—

She turned away from the thought, refusing to finish it. Glancing around, she reviewed the room for options. They were limited at best. The room's large window looked promising—until she pushed back the curtain and looked outside. The dismal night had given way to an equally dismal day.

Gray rain fell from an overcast sky, collecting in half-frozen puddles on the icy, muddy ground. The dark, tangled wood surrounding the house was even denser than she'd imagined, and it stretched out in every direction until her view was obscured by rain and mist. Worse, the house was apparently built on a cliff bluff, and the drop to the rock-hard ground below was almost three full stories. *Even if I made the jump, I'd still have to navigate those woods without a compass, or any sign of the sun to guide me. I'd end up walking in circles until the storm got me. I'll have to find another way out.*

She turned back, narrowing her eyes as she scanned the room. The armoire and the bureau didn't offer much hope, but the rolltop desk held promise. People kept extra sets of keys in desks. People kept maps in desks. In any case, it wouldn't hurt to take a look.

The top was locked as securely as the bedroom door, but the mechanism was much more primitive. It took Lyn only a moment to pick it—one of the perks of having an adopted brother who'd spent time in juvenile detention for breaking into school lockers. But thoughts of her family brought up new concerns.

Last night she'd been too wrapped up in the chaotic events of the evening to give much thought to anything else. She doubted that the police even knew she was missing yet; since the young officer had driven away before Curt had stepped out of the shadows. But eventually they'd find out. And eventually they'd call Corners, her family's east Texas farm, asking if she was there. And when her parents put two and two together, they'd realize what had happened, and start to worry like crazy—

The desk lock sprang open. With a renewed sense of urgency she began to search the desk, looking for something, anything, that might help her escape. She found nothing. Curt was disgustingly efficient in his use of space—except for paper, pens, office files, and the odd paper clip, there was nothing at all in his desk. "Damn, why'd I teach him to be organized?" she muttered as she pushed aside the neatly labeled files.

She opened every drawer and rifled through it, finding nothing . . . until she reached the bottom drawer. It wouldn't open. Must be stuck, she thought, giving it an extra pull. Still it didn't budge. She was about to give it a third yank when she discovered it had an extra lock on it, in addition to the one on the desk. And extra locks meant something valuable, and possibly something useful. . . .

Her thoughts ended abruptly as a loud knock pounded the door. "Lyn!" called a deep baritone voice from the other side.

Damn, she thought as she looked from the door to the locked drawer. There was no time to open it. She'd have to bide her time, and wait until—

The knock sounded again. "Lyn! Do you hear me? I'm coming in."

"Not yet. I'm . . . still dressing," she called back as she shut the desk drawers, trying to be quick and quiet at once. Just a few seconds, that was all she needed. She finished the drawers and pulled down the rolltop. Just one second more . . .

She heard the key turn in the door. She yanked down the rolltop, only to find that the broken lock kept her from pulling it back in place. She pushed it down as far as it would go, praying he didn't notice the change. Then, in the millisecond remaining, she stepped away from the incriminating desk and pulled off her sweater, holding it in front of her. She'd told him she was still dressing. Better give him some proof.

The door opened and Curt strode into the room. He'd changed into work jeans and a forest-green wool shirt, and his expression was dark as thunder. He wasn't a man who liked to be kept waiting.

He wasn't a man who was easily fooled either.

"What's going on?" he demanded.

She stiffened, pressing the sweater closer against her breasts. "I'm dressing."

"For an hour? I don't think so."

He headed for the desk. Lyn's heart stopped—and started a second later when he passed the desk, heading for the window. He tested the window latch, apparently relieved to find it locked. "I was afraid you'd try to use this window to escape, and end up breaking your pretty little neck."

It annoyed her to think he didn't believe she was capable of figuring that out for herself. "I'm not stupid."

"Neither am I," he said as he left the window. He walked back to her, towering over her like a dark mountain. "I know it doesn't take an hour for you to get showered and dressed. You're up to something, Angel. What is it?"

She wanted to be cool, icy, but her body made that impossible. Sexual heat sizzled between them like an electric current, making her aware of him on every level possible. His gaze raked over her naked shoulders, branding her.

Images of what they'd been doing an hour ago filled her mind, shaming her, exciting her. Images of what she'd been doing for the past hour also filled her mind, including his anger if he found out she'd been rifling through his desk. "I'm sorry I took so long," she said carefully. "If you give me a minute, I'll finish dressing."

The corner of his hard mouth edged up in a humorless smile. "You're apologizing. Now I know something's up."

He put his finger under her chin and brought her eyes up to meet his. Even his touch was ice. She shivered, realizing there was no compassion in his dark gaze, and not an ounce of pity. She was looking into the eyes of a hard, ruthless stranger—a stranger perfectly capable of committing murder. Until this moment she hadn't believed he'd done it—not in her soul, where it mattered.

Dr. Osbourne had told her that people could change what they were, but not *who* they were. She'd been clinging to that belief, remembering the man that Curt had once been. But maybe, just maybe, she was seeing him as he really was for the first time in her life. Maybe she'd been wrong about him from the start. And if that were true, then everything she believed about love and faith was a lie—a cheap, empty, useless lie.

"No more games, Angel. You've got thirty seconds," he bit out as he turned away and left the room, leaving the door open behind him. "Time's running out."

It already has, she thought as she crumbled to the bed, defeated.

"You're not eating much," Curt commented as he watched Lyn push her eggs and bacon around the plate he'd put in front of her.

"I'm not very hungry." She set her fork down and shoved the remains of her breakfast toward him across the kitchen pass-through counter. "Guess I'm done—unless you're going to hold that gun on me to force me to eat."

Curt looked down at the revolver he'd stuck in his belt. He'd put it there to remind her—and himself—that he was the one who was in control around here. She was his hostage, his captive, his prisoner—she was only alive because he needed her, and she'd stay alive only so long as she followed orders.

He wanted to make her see the man he was, and not confuse him with some starry-eyed kid she'd once had a crush on. He needed to make her fear him, loathe him if that's what it took, and—most of all—stay well clear of him. So far, his plan seemed to be working beautifully.

So why aren't I happier about it?

He poured himself another mug of thick, black coffee, wishing like hell that his hostage could be anyone in the world instead of her. But wishing got you nowhere. He knew that like he knew his own name. "All right, if you're not going to eat, then tell me about the computer array."

"I've already told you once."

"I dig holes in the ground for a living, remember? Now, you'll do what I tell you, un-less—he rested his hand strategically on the butt of his weapon—"you want to face the consequences."

The look she gave him was pure hellfire. Damn, she had courage. It was ridiculous to admire her for it, especially since it was causing him a world of trouble, but he couldn't help himself. Just like he couldn't help himself from noticing the way her drying hair curled in soft tendrils against her cheeks, or the way her oversized sweater kept slipping off to bare one softly rounded shoulder, or from remembering how it had felt to hold her in his arms, to touch her, smell her, taste her—

He took a deep drag of his coffee. "Tell me about the array. Why don't you think anyone tampered with it?"

"Because it's impossible. The whole system's built on a closed-end kinematic modeling platform. It's an interactive design—there's no way to modify a part of it without that change echoing through the whole digital matrix."

"So it *can* be changed," Curt said, fastening on her admission.

"Well, technically yes," she conceded. "We have to go in for routine maintenance and soft-ware upgrades. But it's an incredibly intricate process—you not only have to know a battery of computer security codes, you have to know the internal design of the system, which is exclusive to Guardian. It couldn't be done by some average schmuck off the streets."

"Thanks for the flattering description," he said dryly, lifting a wry eyebrow.

Her quick smile disarmed him. It was bad enough wanting her sexually, but her mischievous grin blasted through every one of his defenses. She had courage, integrity, *and* a sense of humor. Combined, they added up to a package as dangerous as the dynamite he'd handled for the wildcat drilling operation.

She thought he was guilty. She'd run to the cops if he gave her even half a chance. And he needed her to stay with him. He needed her so much. . . . "So you think one of the Guardian employees might have done it?"

"I don't think anything of the sort," she replied confidently, but the way she toyed with her spoon told a different story.

"Something on your mind, Lyn?"

She started to shake her head, but hesitated, her innate honesty getting the better of her. "It's just that when the policewoman showed me the tape, I remember thinking it was a little . . . choppy."

"Like it was fake?"

"Like it was choppy," she corrected. "The array was designed to digitize stationary objects, not moving ones, but it still records . . . whatever it sees."

Like a murder, he thought sourly. Who was

he kidding? Whoever killed Saltsgaver and framed him was good—too good to get caught by a technical glitch. He shook his head and took another swallow of coffee, wishing like hell that he'd spent the last few years learning something besides crude oil and cash flow. "Could you have done it?"

He'd meant it as a rhetorical question, to gauge the level of technical expertise needed to tamper with the array. That wasn't how she took it. Her smile died and she froze, her eyes taking on a wary, hunted expression.

"I guess I should have expected it," she said quietly. "I knew you'd try to pin your crime on someone. Why not me?"

Curt nearly choked on his coffee. "That is the craziest . . . look, I needed your car, and I needed your smarts. That's why I brought you here. Period."

"Fine," she fired back. "I've told you what I know about the array and you've got your own car in the garage. I've done everything you asked of me. So I think it's only fair . . ." She paused, lifting her chin determinedly. "I think it's only fair that you let me go."

She had courage, integrity, and humor. She was also stark raving mad. "Not a chance. I'm not about to let you drive out of here and straight to the nearest police station."

"But I won't go to the police," she promised as she pushed back her stool and stood up.

Save 85% Off The Cover Price on 4 *Loveswept* Romances

Get 4 Loveswept Romances

For The Low Introductory Price

Of Just $ **1.99** *

*Plus shipping & handling, sales tax in New York, and GST Canada.

Titles you
receive may
differ from
those shown
here, but
will be
the latest
Loveswept
selections

No Risk. No obligation to purchase. No commitment.

"I'll drive back to Fort Worth without making a single stop, I swear it."

"Like you swore you wouldn't try to escape at the service station last night?" he said icily.

She paled, realizing she'd strayed into dangerous territory. "That was . . . different."

"Right. I was more gullible then," he acknowledged as he walked past her out of the kitchen.

"Please, I'm not asking for myself," she pleaded as she followed him into the living room. "I'm thinking about my family. When they find out I'm missing they're going to be worried sick. You know them, Curt. They don't deserve that kind of distress."

He stopped by the fireplace and threw a log on the already well-stocked fire. "Yeah, well, we've all got our problems."

The flames crackled and sputtered. The sharp, spicy scent of burning cedar filled his nostrils, but it might have smelled like old tennis shoes for all he cared. He felt dead inside, as if his whole body had suddenly been turned to stone. It was kinder than letting him feel . . .

When he'd first arrived at the oil rig, he'd looked in horror at the poverty around him—the dreadful conditions of a jungle town with too few jobs and too many mouth to feed. He'd tried his best to do something about it, but he was only one man. He'd petitioned the government for help. The only thing the government had sent back were endless forms and empty promises. For months he continued to try to make a difference on his own, but he was no match for centuries of poverty and ignorance.

In the end he'd given up, and hardened his heart against the suffering of the people. He'd learned how to turn off his feelings, to ignore the appalling horrors and injustices. He'd told himself he was doing it to survive, but that wasn't the whole truth. He was doing it because he was tired of fighting a losing battle. And he was doing it because, with Lyn out of his life, there didn't seem much point to fighting any battles. *Never look back.* . . .

He heard a soft sniff beside him. Out of the corner of his eye he looked over and saw the shine of wetness on her cheeks. *Hell.* He'd faced down a mob of rioting workers at the rig. He'd gone one-on-one with a convicted killer in a knife fight. He'd defused a bomb that had been meant to blow up one of his wells. He'd pulled Benny out of a roaring oil-fire blaze. He'd faced more dangers than most men come up against in a lifetime, and survived. But he didn't even begin to have the courage he needed to face her tears.

He took a step toward her, and halted. Last night, when she'd started crying, he'd taken her in his arms and comforted her. It had been an unusually selfless act on his part, but the sad truth was that his good deed was the result of fatigue rather than character. Last night he'd simply been too damn tired to do anything *but* comfort her. This morning, however, was another matter. His usually unyielding control was already strained to the breaking point by sexual frustration. If he touched her now he wasn't sure what would happen.

Groaning inwardly, he shoved his hands into his jeans pockets. "Look, I'm sorry you're upset. But there's nothing I can do about—"

She cried harder.

To hell with control. In two strides he was next to her, wrapping her in his strong, protective embrace. Her slim body trembled like a leaf in the wind, and every shiver rocked through him like an earthquake. You're a damn fool, he thought, knowing full well that he was heading for a mountain of trouble. But that didn't matter. She was frightened and alone, and she needed his comfort. She needed him, by God, and for once in his life he wasn't going to let her down.

"It'll be all right," he promised gently, pulling her close against his chest. She felt so fragile, like a helpless, baby bird. He smiled slightly, thinking how she'd hate that comparison. "Somehow, I'll make it work out all right."

She said something, but the words were lost in a soggy muffle against his chest. He set his

cheek against her silky hair and hugged her
tight, feeling a tenderness so fierce, it robbed
his breath. During the years he'd held dozens
of women in his arms, but not one of them
moved him like she did. Her sweet, brave spirit
had reached down to his core, healing the dark
and hurting places in his soul. He closed his
eyes and breathed in the soft scent of her hair,
knowing he was skirting dangerously close to
the edge of disaster. Six years ago he'd found
the strength to give her up. He doubted he'd
find that strength again.

She moved in his arms, tilting her face up
to his. Her blue eyes shimmered with unshed
tears, but her gaze was clear and unafraid. "You
aren't as bad as you pretend to be, are you?"

"Don't bet on it," he growled, his control
finally breaking as he lowered his mouth to
hers.

He'd planned to make it a chaste kiss, just a
taste of her before he let her go forever. His
good intentions exploded as soon as his lips
touched hers. She was soft and lush and so
damn sweet, it made his head spin. Kissing her
was like getting drunk on the finest wine, an
irresistible indulgence. But he had to resist it,
for her sake. Groaning, he reluctantly started
to pull back. It wasn't until he felt her fingers
thread through the hair at the nape of his neck
that he realized she was kissing him back.

The world turned to fire. Tenderness

burned away in white-hot heat, exploding through them like living fire. He plundered her mouth, taking his forbidden taste—a taste she impossibly seemed to want to give him as much as he needed to take it. Six years of wanting erupted inside him. It was madness, but it was a madness that made more sense than anything else in his cold, empty life. He kissed her harder and fiercer than before, starving for the sweet hunger of her lips, for the joy and acceptance he'd never found anywhere but in her arms.

For six long years he'd lived without her, giving his passion to his work, pretending that sex was the same as true, honest love. For six long years he'd been living a lie. He slid his arms beneath her sweater and ran his hands over the smooth, naked, achingly familiar length of her back. He wanted to claim her body and her heart, to win back the love that time and circumstances had ripped from their lives, to heal the hurts inside her as she'd once healed his. Fate had sent her back to him and he was never letting go of her, never. . . .

"I didn't plan on this," she said, her words a husky whisper against his cheek.

"Neither did I," he breathed as he trailed searing kisses along the side of her neck. "But I'm glad it happened, Angel. I'm glad."

She moaned, her eyes drifting shut as she shuddered under the double caress of his words and his kisses. "I mean," she continued breath-lessly. "I want you to know it's nothing personal."

His deep chuckle echoed through her like thunder. "Sweetheart, this is as personal as it gets."

She gave her head a short, distressed shake. "I'm not talking about the kiss."

"Then what . . . ?" His sentence died as he felt the hard reality of the nose of an automatic being pressed into his stomach.

NINE

His curse blistered her ears.

"I didn't have a choice," Lyn said as she slowly backed away. She held the gun in both hands. It still shook. "I just wanted—"

"You wanted to get even," Curt fired back, his jaw hardening to a stony grimace. "Congratulations, Angel. Nobody's done me like that in a long, long time."

"That's not . . ." she began, but the arctic look in his eyes froze her to silence. He hated her. She didn't blame him. Her lips were still swollen from the bruising passion of his kiss, a passion that continued to throb through her body. Whatever else he was guilty of, he'd meant that kiss. And she'd used it as a cheap sham to steal his gun. She winced, feeling a little sick inside at what she'd done. *But I didn't have a choice!*

"I just want my car keys," she said aloud, fighting to keep both her voice and the gun level. "Give them to me or I'll shoot you."

His eyes narrowed to an obsidian gleam. "Right."

He thinks I haven't got the guts. Belatedly, she realized he might be right. The thought of shooting him with his kiss still hot on her lips, and the memory of his fingers searing her skin . . .

Ruthlessly, she shoved the confusion out of her heart and mind. He was a criminal, a kidnapper, and almost certainly a murderer. His kiss was just another deception. It had to be. She lifted her chin, meeting his chilling gaze with a confidence she didn't even begin to feel. "I *will* shoot you," she promised evenly.

A disarming grin sliced his dark, dangerous expression. "Maybe. A woman who uses sex as effectively as you do is capable of anything. But I'm a betting man, Angel, and I'm betting that you wouldn't shoot a man in cold blood. Even if that man is me."

"You'd lose," she warned.

His smile dissolved. "I've already lost," he said cryptically as he slowly, cautiously extended his hand. "Come on, Lyn. Give me the gun."

"No," she said, or tried to. It was getting hard to breathe. Her lungs felt tight, like a great weight was pressing down on them. The revolver felt heavy in her hand, and cold as death. And Curt's obsidian eyes burned into hers like living fire.

She knew what a bullet could do to a man —she'd seen it when she'd lived on the streets. Once she'd seen a man bleed to death in front of her. The thought of causing that kind of destruction to another human being, especially to someone she'd once loved . . .

But she couldn't think of that. She couldn't give in, not now. She owed it to Salty, and to herself. She had the gun, which meant she had the advantage, even if it was a shaky one at best. *I'm a betting man, too, Curt Brennermen, and I know that a savvy bluff can be just as effective as a handful of aces.* She straightened her shoulders and met his dark gaze with a cool, blue stare. "You're not much of a gambler, Curt Brennermen. You've got to know that I'd jump at the chance to shoot you, in cold blood or otherwise. Now, give me those keys, or I will shoot. I promise."

"Guess there's only one way to find out," he said with lethal softness.

He took a step toward her. The air sizzled between them. Damn, she thought, why do they call it stalemate? There's nothing stale about this. She watched his eyes, feeling their midnight power surge through her like a raw electric current. Awareness ripped through her with the force of a bullet, adding to the already potent arousal of his kiss. His dark gaze consumed her, mesmerizing her, searing her from the inside out. At that moment she wasn't sure whether he wanted to kill her or make love to her. At that moment she wasn't sure she cared which.

For years she'd kept her emotions safely under control. But in a matter of hours Curt had ripped her open, unleashing all the fear and hate and, yes, love she'd kept bottled up inside her. The rising tide of emotion was tearing her apart.

"Please," she said, her voice shaking with strain, "don't make me choose—"

Suddenly he lunged at her, grabbing for the gun. Startled, she staggered back and caught her knee on the arm of the couch. The move unbalanced her, toppling her backward onto the plush cushions. And as she fell she pulled the trigger.

The explosion shattered the silence. Stunned, Lyn struggled up from the cushions she'd been flung against by the force of the shot. She blinked, focusing her eyes on Curt's still-standing form. "Thank God," she breathed in a relief too great to hide. "I missed—"

Then she saw the blood.

"No!" She ran to him. Blood dripped down his right arm and the right leg of his jeans.

Panicked, she couldn't see where she'd hit him. "Oh God, where—"

"My side," he said, his voice thick with barely controlled pain. "Only a flesh wound, I think."

"But there's so much blood. . . ."

"Happens when you shoot someone," he said with a weak laugh. He staggered to the couch and sat heavily on the arm, smiling at her with a ghost of his wolfish grin. "You're a hell of a shot, lady."

"Don't you *dare* make macho jokes," she warned as she bent to examine his wound. The bullet had torn a hole through the fabric of his shirt near the hip. She swallowed, trying to remain calm as she yanked the bottom of his shirt from his jeans. "I think you're right. It's only a flesh—"

She drew in her breath in a shocked hiss. The bullet had torn across the side of his abdomen. The wound wasn't deep enough to hit any vital organs, but it was serious just the same. New blood was pumping through the cut with every beat of his heart. If she didn't stop the flow soon . . .

"Where do you keep your dishtowels?"

He stared at her, puzzled. "Hell of a time to clean the kitchen," he muttered.

"I need to put pressure on the wound," she explained, exasperated. "To stop the bleeding."

"Oh. Top drawer on right—"

She was off before he finished the sentence. She ran into the kitchen and opened the drawer, scooping up all the towels in the stack. Returning, she saw that he'd unbuttoned his shirt and was attempting to shrug it off his shoulders. Every moment made him wince with new pain.

"Stop that!" she said, feeling his pain as if it were her own. Bending down, she pressed a towel against his wound, trying to disguise her distress at how quickly the cream-colored material turned to bright crimson. *Don't panic, Lyn. Keep it together, for his sake.*

Summoning her courage, she forced a confident smile on her face. "I can stop the flow for now. But we'd still better get you to a hospital as soon as—"

"No hospitals," he interrupted, shaking his head like an angry lion. "No doctors. They'll call the police—"

"They'll keep you alive!"

"No doctors. I—" He winced sharply, then sighed raggedly as he fought back a spasm of pain. With what was obviously a tremendous effort, he lifted his head to meet her gaze. "Please, Angel. No doctors. No matter what happens."

The pain in his eyes cut her in two. He was a powerful man, but his strength was fading by the minute. She could feel it draining out of him like water through a sieve. Or blood from a wound. Biting her lip, she raised her hand to cup his cheek, but drew back when she saw the red stain of his blood on her fingers. *Once she'd seen a man bleed to death.*

"Curt, I think this wound is serious. If it's not treated, you might . . ." Her voice dwindled to a whisper. She dropped her eyes, unable to meet his gaze. If he died, it would be by her hand. She'd have killed him. . . .

"Lyn, look at me."

His voice was low and racked with pain, but it still carried the absolute authority of a man in control. Unable to resist, she raised her head to meet his dark gaze, expecting to see the condemnation and fear she already felt in her heart. Instead, she saw forgiveness, and a concern so intense it made her weak.

"It's not your fault," he said huskily, his voice fading with his strength. He raised his hand and laced his fingers through hers, pulling it against his heart. "My fault. Shouldn't have gone at you like that. Don't blame yoursel—"

His words were cut short by another spasm of pain. He winced sharply and sagged against the back of the couch. She cried aloud and frantically pressed the towel harder against his wound. She couldn't tell if it was doing any good. There was so much blood already, so much. "Dammit, I'm taking you to a hospital whether you like it or not."

"Don't think so," he said as his eyes drifted shut. "You still don't have the car keys, 'member?"

She grasped his shoulders, pulling him back to a sitting position. Already his body felt like deadweight. She shivered, too frightened to hide it. "Curt, tell me where the keys are! I'll . . . I'll just go and get some bandages, I promise."

"You're a lousy liar," he muttered, falling against her shoulder. "But your skin smells great. Like summer. You always smell like Texas summer."

"You're delirious."

"Not yet," he muttered into the curve of her neck. His words were beginning to slur together, a sign that he was fast losing consciousness. As if in slow motion he raised his pain-clouded eyes to hers. "Promise. No doctors."

"No," she said in a voice barely above a whisper. "I can't promise. I don't want you to die."

"Not too crazy about it myself," he admitted with a harsh, ragged chuckle. With a final effort he lifted his fingers and wiped away tears she didn't even know she was crying. "Don't cry, little Angel. I'm not worth—"

He pitched forward into her arms, unconscious.

"Curt!" She struggled against the sudden overbalancing weight of his heavy, muscular form. Grabbing his shoulders, she shook him, but Curt was out cold, unconscious from the pain or the loss of blood, probably both. Stifling her panic, she gritted her teeth and summoned up every ounce of her strength. She lowered him gently to the cushions. His skin was as pale as a ghost's, and when she pressed her hand to his chest, his skin felt warm and clammy.

She swallowed, fighting back a wave of despair. No matter what he'd done, no matter what he'd been accused of, she couldn't let him die. *Forgive me, Salty.*

The next hour was a blur. Lyn was in motion every second, working partly from instinct, and partly from the facts she'd gleaned from helping her brother Micah study for his premed exams. The combined knowledge was sporadic at best, but it got her past the worst of it.

She cleaned the wound as best she could, using the towels and a small first-aid kit she found in the kitchen pantry. The bullet had traveled through muscle but missed his bone, making a complete, if messy, exit through his side. That was the good news. The bad news was that even without the complications of possible lead poisoning, it was a very nasty injury. By the time she'd cleaned and bandaged the wound, he'd lost a considerable amount of blood. But his color seemed to be returning, and when she placed her palm on his chest, his heartbeat felt sure and strong. She examined his bandage a final time, then sank to the floor beside the couch, breathing a silent, exhausted prayer of relief that his crisis was over.

She couldn't have been more wrong.

She picked up a cedar log and tossed it on the fire, watching the spray of bright sparks fly up the chimney toward heaven. The new warmth and spicy cedar scent curled around her like a comforting blanket, but even the cheerful fire couldn't improve her spirits. He'd been out for almost two hours, would be waking up soon.

And what happens when he does? an inner voice questioned.

She turned around and looked to where Curt's long, lean body was sprawled across the couch. Though he was still unconscious, his breathing was even, and his color was returning, telling her that he was out of danger. She wished she could say the same for herself. The hard lines of his face were softened by slumber and his gold hair was tumbled across his forehead, making him look young and achingly vulnerable. A tenderness as fierce as passion rose within her. *He's a fugitive, a kidnapper, and you just shot him in self-defense. He's a dangerous man, a killer, who's betrayed you not once*

*but twice. A smart woman would leave now, before
he wakes up, and gets the chance to fill her head
with more lies.*

Without taking her gaze from Curt, she
reached under her sweater for the hard shape
of the gun. She'd taken out the bullets—knowing she'd never again be able to point a loaded
weapon at another human being—but the gun
was evidence and she intended to keep it.

The pocket beneath the gun held something far more useful to her. She reached into
it, fingering the car keys she'd found a quarter
hour before in one of the kitchen drawers.
Curt hadn't gone to much trouble to hide
them—but then, he probably wasn't expecting
her to have the chance to search for them. In
any case, the keys gave her the power to leave
this house and her unconscious captor behind.
She could drive to the nearest police station,
tell them the location of Curt's house, and have
him in custody before evening. She'd have
done her duty to Salty, to justice, and to herself. She could put this whole horrible episode
behind her.

And possibly help send an innocent man to
his death.

She wrapped her arms around her middle,
as if physical strength could contain the storm
winds of uncertainty that ripped through her
soul. Logically there was no question of what
she should do and whom she should believe.

Curt's actions from the beginning had been those of a guilty man. She'd seen the tape of his crime—a tape that could have only been counterfeited by one of her coworkers, people she'd trusted far more than she would ever trust him. He had a history of betraying her. There was no reason on earth why she should even consider believing him. No reason, except for the way she'd felt when she thought he was dying, how she'd have willingly traded the whole of her own life to keep him alive for another minute . . .

He stirred restlessly in his sleep. "Angel?"

She stiffened, fighting against the almost unbearable urge to rush to his side. She lifted her chin, setting her sights on the front door. She had to leave. Now, before she did something she'd regret for the rest of her probably very short life—

"Angel, where are you?" he moaned.

Damn him, she thought as she took a step toward the couch. And damn me for being the world's biggest fool. She moved closer, until she was near enough to speak to him in a low, soothing tone. "You're going to be all right, Curt. You're strong and healthy, and well on your way to recovery. I'm going now, but I want you to know that I wouldn't leave if I thought you were in any danger—"

Her words died as he thrashed his head back and forth, like a man caught in a net. His unbuttoned shirt fell open, revealing a wide expanse of his muscular, fur-dusted chest. Lyn swallowed, feeling a very different kind of emotion rip through her. *He's plenty healthy— and so am I, unfortunately. I'd better leave now, before I'm the one who's in danger. . . .*

"Get the mustard," he muttered thickly.

She frowned, annoyed in spite of her anxiety that he could dream of her and condiments in the same breath. Dr. Osbourne could probably deduce some deep Freudian meaning from the combination. She, however, was merely insulted. *Wonderful. I'm right up there with hot dogs and ham sandwiches—*

"Get the bastard!" he cried, making her realize that she'd misunderstood his last word. He tossed his head, his brow creased in dark anguish. "Got to find him. He killed Salty."

Lyn went still, her mouth growing dry as dust. "Curt," she said carefully, "*you* killed Salty."

"Get the bastard," he repeated, clearly not hearing her. "He killed once. Might hurt Lyn . . ."

"No," she breathed, shaking her head. For a moment she wasn't sure whom she was talking to, himself or her. He was still unconscious —there was no denying that he was speaking the truth. And yet she did resist it, fighting against it like a bird trying to free itself from a hunter's snare.

She'd battled against trusting him from the beginning, believing the worst of him, refusing to consider even the possibility that he might be telling the truth. Dr. Osbourne had said that she had a problem with trust, but it was more than that. It was Curt she couldn't allow herself to believe in. She had to keep a wall between them, battle to keep him at a safe distance because—

Her thoughts ended as he moved, thrashing his head so hard against the back of the couch, she feared he might hurt himself. "She doesn't believe me. . . ."

"Yes, she does," Lyn admitted softly, kneeling down beside him. "I should have listened to you hours ago, and would have if I hadn't . . . Curt, will you quit moving around?" she chided as she reached out to steady him. "If you keep this up you'll tear—"

Her words died as she touched the bare skin of his shoulder. His returning color wasn't a sign of health at all. The man was burning up with fever!

TEN

She laid two fingers against the side of his throat, taking his pulse. The rapid, shallow beats frightened her almost as much as his loss of blood had. At this rate his heart would exhaust his already weakened body until he wouldn't be able to recover. She had to bring down his temperature quickly, before the heat used up what remained of his limited strength.

She turned quickly and reached for the medical kit, but stopped as the sharp metal shapes of the gun and the car keys bit into her midriff. She pulled both of them out and laid them on the coffee table. She wished she could toss them both across the bloody room!

Once again she battled to save him, but this time the fight was fiercer, and longer. She'd never studied this portion of Micah's medical texts, and she hadn't the faintest idea of what to do, except that she had to bring down his temperature quickly without shocking his system.

Using the scissors she'd found in the medical kit, she cut away the remains of his ruined shirt, peeling the stiff, blood-crusted material away from his body. Then she sponged his torso with a combination of lukewarm water and disinfectant. Everywhere she touched, his skin was hot, burning. Stifling her panic, she sat on the couch and cradled his head in her lap as she washed down his limbs. *I can't let him die. Not before . . .*

Before what? her mind questioned as the thought dwindled off.

"Nothing," she muttered aloud, shying away from a thought that frightened her almost as much as his fever. She picked up the cloth and drew it across his chest. His body was fit and iron hard and she took comfort in his strength, hoping it was enough to see him through this new crisis. Encouraged, she dipped her towel in the bowl and started to dab his chest. "You know," she said, smiling bravely, "this would be a lot easier if you were a ninety-eight-pound weakling. You're heavy."

He mumbled something, but she couldn't understand it. Worried, she moved her hand until it pressed against his heart, trying to take comfort in the slowing beat. The drop in his heart rate could mean that his fever was breaking, but it could just as easily mean he was losing his fight. Curt was strong, but physical strength was only half the battle. A man had to have the will to live, and she wasn't sure he had that will. "Curt, I can't do this alone," she confessed as she wrung out the towel and stroked it down his arm. "You have to help—"

Her voice evaporated as she saw the scar.

It was nearly six inches long, a bold, jagged cut along his upper arm. She laid aside the towel and fingered the old and terrible wound, feeling confused beyond measure. He hadn't had that scar seven years ago; she remembered every inch of his body with a complete and sometimes very inconvenient clarity. He must have gotten it during his years in South America. But that didn't make any sense.

He'd written her only a few times during their first year apart, but when he had, his letters had been filled with glowing descriptions of his great new job and his fabulous new life. She had imagined him sitting on a sun-drenched beach, sipping a piña colada as he watched the waves break against the shore. After his final letter, she'd added a couple of scantily clad babes to the picture.

But the ugly scar on his arm didn't fit into that picture-postcard existence. Neither did the one near his left nipple, or the thin, puckered scar on his stomach. She'd spent enough time on the streets to know what the results of a vicious knife fight looked like. Horrified, she

realized that sometime in the past Curt had
been in a battle for his life. And all this time
she'd thought he was sitting on some stupid
beach, making time with bimbos—

He jerked his head, startling her back to
reality. The past would have to wait—she had
way too much to deal with in the present. She
dunked the towel again and drew it across his
chest. "Don't you dare die on me, Curt," she
ordered as she cooled his fiery skin. "You owe
me a hell of an explanation."

For what seemed an eternity she rinsed out
the towel and bathed his skin, hoping and praying she was doing the right thing. When she
was done she got a Navaho blanket and tucked
it securely around him. She bent over him as
she pulled the blanket up around his chin, staring into his calm but still-unconscious face. I
don't know if I've done any good at all, she
thought, brushing back tears of frustration. I
don't know how to help him.

Yes, you do, said a small voice inside her.
Give him a reason to live.

She knelt down and tenderly pushed a lock
of hair off his forehead. "I don't know if you
can hear me. In fact, I'm pretty sure you can't.
But I don't want you to die. There's so many
things I want to tell you. You remember that
bay mare I used to ride? You named her
Doomsday because you said she was too bad-
tempered to die before then. Well, she's still

alive, and just as ornery as ever. I used to imagine our son riding—"

She stopped, fighting a surge of emotion so powerful, it almost overwhelmed her. "I know there's not going to be any son. I know you don't feel that way about me anymore. But couldn't you pretend, just for a minute? Couldn't you pretend just long enough to stay alive . . . ?"

For a long moment the only sounds in the room were the sizzle of the logs on the fire, and the pounding of her heart. She lifted her head, noticing for the first time that the rain outside had stopped and the storm was beginning to break up. She'd thought only minutes had passed, but it must have been hours. She pushed back her sweat-dampened locks, beginning to feel the drag of her own exhaustion. *I can't take much more of this, I can't—*

She sensed a slight, barely discernible shift in his breathing. His breaths seemed to be growing deeper, more regular. He'd slipped into a what appeared to be a restless but sound sleep. She felt his brow, and had to bite her lip from crying aloud with relief. It was cool and dry to her touch. He was going to be all right.

Curt faded in and out of consciousness for the rest of Friday afternoon and through the long night that followed. Lyn watched him like a hawk, almost never leaving his side except to get more towels or make him a dinner of canned beef broth she'd found in one of the kitchen cabinets. She spoon-fed him like a child, feeling the thrill of victory each time he took a weak sip. She didn't know how much he would remember. She didn't care. He was alive, and that was all that mattered. She'd kept him alive.

Near dawn she took time out for a brief shower, but was back at his side in less than fifteen minutes. As the morning dragged on she listened to a small radio she'd found on one of the living-room shelves, hoping to catch a newscast, but heard nothing except posturing politicians pledging that they would spare no expense to find Curt Brennermen and bring him in for questioning. Eventually she switched off the radio, depressed by the one-sided newscasts and by the endless stream of country songs about lost loves and aching hearts, which hit way too close to home for comfort.

Giving up, she returned to Curt's sleeping figure and laid her palm against his now cool forehead. She bent down and placed a soft, reverent kiss on his sleeping lips. Then she went over to the chair beside the couch and collapsed into its leather cushions as her eyes drifted shut in her own troubled dreams.

◈———————◈

It was evening. The storm had finally ended and the angry clouds had begun to roll away toward the east. In the far west the sun had found a slim break in the sky, shining a last copper ray across the darkening heavens. The dying sunlight poured through the wide picture window, casting a streak of fire across the figure of the man who stood in the middle of the living room. Startled by the unexpected light, he turned and faced the final brilliance, until the dark clouds came together like a closing hand and snuffed out the last of the day. A minute of light and a long night of darkness, he thought as he stared out at the gathering gloom. Probably better if the light had never come at all.

No, not that, his heart whispered. *You don't wish that.*

"But I should," he muttered as he glanced over at the slim, silent figure asleep in a chair by the fireplace.

He headed to the front door, his boots making barely a whisper against the soft carpet. Years ago in the jungle he'd learned the hunter's walk—though he'd been the prey more times than he cared to admit. Being pursued by the Fort Worth police was a cakewalk compared with being chased by his competitor's beefy, mustachioed hit man with a razor-sharp machete and a bad attitude. Still, he recalled the basic tricks of the trade. Always walk downwind. Always treat your shoes and feet like solid gold. And always, always travel alone.

So much for rule number three . . .

He rubbed his newly shaven chin, studying the small collection of knapsacks piled by the front door. The bags contained enough food and clothing to last him a couple of weeks on the road. He figured he'd head for Mexico— Benny had friends who would get him across the border. Out of the States he could contact his business associates in South America. They had an underground communication network that—while it didn't exactly break the law— tended to bend it to its limit. He'd get in touch with Benny, and together they'd figure out this computerized con job. It was a good plan, except for one loose end. One single, beautiful, currently-asleep-in-a-chair-by-the-fireplace loose end.

He bent down, checking the bags for the third time in less than an hour. She'll be better off with the police, he told himself. They'll be all over her like a cheap suit; the murderer won't have a chance to get to her, even if he thinks she knows too much. Besides, she's told you all she knows about the array. There's no reason to keep her with you anymore.

No reason except one.

He straightened quickly, and winced from the sudden stab of pain in his side. Like getting kicked in the gut by a mule, he thought with a grim smile. He'd had worse—much worse—but the pain of this wound seemed to cut deeper. *If it is the wound that's hurting.*

A rustle by the fireplace caught his attention. She was waking up. He looked at the equipment by the door, wondering again why he didn't just throw it in his truck and go before she woke up. But he couldn't just leave her with nothing but a hastily scribbled note. He fingered the set of car keys in his pocket—ones he'd retrieved from the coffee table along with the empty gun. Clearly, she'd had the chance to leave him, but had stayed to save his life. He owed her. Besides, the thought of leaving her for a second time with nothing more than a letter turned his stomach. She deserved better. She always had.

He walked back to the fireplace and leaned against the mantel, watching as sleep slowly lost its hold on her. Curled up under the Navaho blanket with her hair all crazy, she looked about as dangerous as a newborn kitten. Some kitten, he thought as he fanned his fingers over his side, feeling the bandage under his chamois shirt. Hellcat is more like it. The lady was more trouble than a case of dynamite.

But he didn't regret a single minute of the last twenty-four hours, even if Lyn had spent the major portion of that time looking at him like he'd just crawled out from under the nearest rock. God knows, if he'd had the whole thing to do over again, he'd have done everything exactly the same.

Well, maybe not everything . . .

She turned on her side, then made a soft, kittenish sigh as she burrowed deeper under the blanket. Apparently sleep wasn't ready to give her up just yet. *Neither am I,* he thought as a wave of desire caught him off guard. His gaze fastened on the sweet curves hidden beneath the cover, the slim, deceptively innocent-looking body that could make him burn hotter than an oil-field fire. *Take her with you,* his mind whispered. *She believes you. You heard her say so while you were feverish. You could be with her every day—and every night. You could keep her with you in Mexico, build a life together until you clear your name. . . .*

And what if I don't clear my name?

He knew the answer. She'd become a fugitive like him—an accessory to Salty's murder because of her association with him. She'd have to live in another country, separated from her family, friends, and all the people she'd grown to love. She could never go home again, even if she wanted to. He couldn't condemn her to that kind of existence, no matter how much he wanted her. No matter how much he needed her. *Better get this over with,* he thought as he gently nudged her leg with the toe of his boot.

While I've still got the strength to. "Lyn, wake up."

She woke with a confused start, fingering the soft blanket that covered her. Where was she? Or more importantly, she thought in alarm as she glanced toward the empty couch, where was—

"I'm over here."

She turned at the sound of his voice. He was leaning against the fireplace mantel with his arms crossed over his chest, watching her with his dark, fathomless eyes. The first thing her sleep-muddled mind registered was that he'd put on a new, buckskin-colored shirt to replace the one she'd shredded. The next was that he looked perfectly healthy, incredibly handsome, and so damn sexy, it made her heart skip a beat. She rubbed her brow, trying to match her memories to the man who stood above her. "I thought I shot you."

"You did," he rumbled, a smile tugging at the corner of his reluctant mouth.

"I di—good Lord!" She leaped up, the blanket slipping into a heap at her feet. "You shouldn't be standing. You should be lying down and—"

"I'm fine."

"Nonsense," she said, placing the back of her hand against his cheek. "You were burning up with fever. You almost died."

"I was nowhere close," he replied, losing

his battle with his grin. "Once you stopped the bleeding, I was out of danger. Calm down, will you? I'm all right."

He looked all right. Hell, he looked a whole lot better than all right. This virile, confident, and incredibly sexy hunk had nothing in common with the unconscious man she'd pulled back from the brink of death. She swallowed. "You . . . you talked while you were unconscious. You said you didn't kill Salty. I'm . . . sorry I didn't believe you before."

"I didn't give you much of a reason," he said in a deep, velvety voice that had a dangerous effect on her heartbeat. "You know, you're taking a risk. I could have been lying."

"You could have," she agreed with a hesitant grin. "But I didn't figure you were that bright."

He reached up and brushed her cheek with a tenderness that seemed to surprise him as much as her. "You saved my life. Whatever else happens, I want you to know I'm grateful."

So am I, she thought, shivering at the almost unbearable intimacy of his touch. She couldn't have borne losing him—not twice, not a final time. It didn't matter that seven years had passed; seven centuries would have been too short. She looked unafraid into the fathomless darkness of his eyes, knowing that whatever mysteries and misdeeds he contained, he also held her heart. He always would. "Curt," she said, finding it unexpectedly difficult to find the breath to form the words, "I need to tell you something."

"I need to tell *you* something." Abruptly he dropped his hand and turned away, walking toward the middle of the living room. He thrust his hand in his pocket and curved the other around the back of his neck. He looked like a man at war with himself—who was losing the battle on all fronts. "This house is built in the Brazos River Valley. It's located about a hundred and fifty miles northwest of Fort Worth. You can get there by heading east on the farm roads until you hit the main highway."

Why is he giving me the surveyor's rundown of his house? she wondered as she left the fireplace. "No offense, Curt, but I'm not interested in buying this place. I doubt I could afford it."

This time he didn't answer her smile. He stood with his back to her, his shoulders a wall of tension. She frowned, now genuinely concerned. What if his fever was returning? What if he was becoming delirious again? "Curt, I think you should sit down for a while."

"No time," he bit out.

Stubborn cowboy, she thought with an indulgent smile. He never could admit that he was made of flesh and blood like the rest of us. Well, that's going to change. I'm going to see to it that he takes proper care of himself—if it kills me. "I know you're anxious to catch Salty's murderer. So am I. But one night's rest won't make a difference. We can start working on it in the morning."

"No, we can't."

His words rang through her like a funeral knell. Suddenly she was frightened—almost as frightened as she'd been when he was sick. She reached up and laid her hand on his taut shoulder, feeling fragile as blown glass and twice as capable of being shattered. "What's going on, Curt?"

He chuckled, a cold, humorless laugh that chilled her to the bone. He turned around and looked down at her, his expression as remote and forbidding as a granite mountain. "Nothing, except that it's your lucky day, Angel," he said as he dug into his other pocket and pulled out her car keys. "I'm giving you your freedom."

ELEVEN

"What do you mean, 'no'?"

"What do you think I mean?" Lyn replied as she turned and sauntered back to the fireplace. "I'm not ready to leave yet."

"Well, that's too damn bad," he bellowed as he followed her back to the mantel. "This isn't open for discussion. Besides, you *shot* me to get these keys, remember?"

"That was an accident," she commented as she bent down to pick up the fallen Navaho blanket and then began to fold it in neat squares. "Anyway, that's part of the reason I'm staying. You're still not completely healed, no matter what you say. You need someone to look after you."

"I need—" He stopped, pressing the heel of his hand to his suddenly throbbing temple. "Lyn, in case you've forgotten, this is still a hostage-kidnapper situation. And when the kidnapper says 'leave,' it's customary for the hostage to obey him."

She tossed the blanket to the couch. "I've never been a hostage before, so I can't be expected to know what the procedure is."

"I'm serious."

"So am I," she flashed back as she whirled to face him. "A friend of mine is dead. I want his murderer caught, and we have a better chance of doing that if we stick together."

It was a sound, logical argument—and there was no way in hell Curt was going to listen to it. His gaze strayed from her determined expression to where the loose sweater had once again fallen to expose her enticing shoulder. The sweater was thick, but the memory of what his hands had explored the other morning seemed to penetrate her clothing like X-ray vision. *I can't be around her for another couple of days. I can't be around her for another couple of hours.*

Forcing himself to sound angry, he snarled, "Face it, I don't *need* you anymore. You've told me all you know about the array. I have my truck, so I don't need your car. And since you know I'm innocent, you won't tell the police where I am. Not that it would make any difference if you did," he added as he nodded toward the pile of bags by the front door. "I'm leaving too."

"You can't," she said, her veneer of composure disintegrating. "You're still hurt, whether you want to admit it or not. Am I just supposed to walk off and forget about you?"

"Why not?" he fired back with a voice cold enough to freeze sunlight. "That's exactly what I'm going to do."

It was a cheap shot, but apparently a very effective one. She winced as if he'd struck her, then dropped her eyes to the floor. *You didn't deserve that, Angel. Hell, you don't deserve any of this. I've got to get you back to your safe little life, before I do something else you don't deserve. . . .*

He tossed the keys on the couch on top of the blanket—the blanket that had been around him when he'd woken up. She'd tucked him in with a tenderness and care of a mother caring for her child. Or a sweetheart caring for her lover. He closed his eyes, flinching from a pain that had nothing to do with his wound.

"I want you to promise me you'll go straight to the police. If Saltsgaver's murderer is one of the people at Guardian, they might come after you—especially once they learn you've been with me. They might think you know too much."

"They'd be amazed at how little I *do* know," she said dryly.

He frowned, puzzled by her words. But then, she'd been one big question mark ever since he'd offered her the keys. Any other woman would have jumped at the chance to save her skin. But not Lyn.

Misguided as it was, she was concerned for his safety. She thought he needed her. And he hated to think how close he'd come to taking advantage of her concern. He picked the keys up from the sofa and held them out to her. "I also want you to take Saltsgaver's gun with you. The police might be able to run some tests on it and find out something about who fired it."

"Besides me?"

His heart turned over at the self-condemnation in her tone. "Babe, it was an accident. I know that."

She lifted her crystal gaze to his. "Were the scars an accident, too?" she asked quietly.

For a moment he didn't know what she was talking about. Then his eyes widened with understanding. The scars—he'd grown so used to them that he no longer noticed they were there, not even when he looked in the mirror. But he'd forgotten about the mirror of Lyn's blue, much-too-innocent eyes.

"Those old things?" he said, counterfeiting a shrug. "I got them bull riding on the rodeo circuit."

"That's not true," she accused. "I would have remembered. We . . . weren't exactly strangers."

No, they weren't. They'd been as close as

two people could get without climbing into the same skin. He grimaced, realizing she probably recalled his body as clearly as . . . well, as he recalled hers. He remembered the sensitive hollow in the small of her back, the mole above her left breast, the tiny appendix scar just above her—

"Okay, I got them in the oil fields," he said, gritting his teeth in an effort to pull himself back to the present. "Some of my competitors didn't like the fact that I paid my workers double what they did. So they sent around a couple of bullyboys to, er, help me change my mind. No big deal."

"Big enough," she said as he gripped the edge of the mantel. "You could have died from wounds like that. You wrote me that you were living in some sort of jungle paradise. Why didn't you tell me the truth?"

Why? Because you and your well-meaning little heart would have jumped on the first available flight to South America—and ruined your life in the process.

Christ, she'd been innocent as a babe. She believed in truth, honor, and all those other fairy tales that he'd given up during his first year in the tropics. He fingered the bandage beneath his shirt, realizing all too clearly that she still did.

He looked down at the pale silk of her hair and the fragile curve of her elegant neck. He'd known men who'd bought and sold women like her for the price of a drink. That part of his life was over, but the memories remained, an indelible stain on his soul. There was nothing left inside him that even approximated those storybook values she believed in.

"You wouldn't have understood," he said truthfully. "You wouldn't have fit in with my life down there—believe me."

"I guess not," she said as she looked down at the fire, her voice unnaturally still. "And I guess it was pretty awful for you getting all those letters from me."

"Yeah, it was," he agreed, surprised that she'd comprehended so quickly. *Awful* didn't begin to cover it. He'd gone through hell every time he'd opened one.

She swallowed, and wiped her hand across her cheek. Good God, was she crying?

"Lyn . . ." He grasped her shoulders, turning her gently to face him. "Hey, there's no reason to get upset. I dealt with it a long time ago."

"Maybe you did," she replied, ruthlessly rubbing her cheek. "But you're not the one who was so green and stupid and . . . damn!" she cried as she pulled away and hid her face in her hands. "You must have laughed your head off every time you got a letter."

"Laughed? What would I laugh about?" he wondered aloud, truly puzzled.

"About the football games. About the so-
rority teas. About getting an 'A' on my first
physics ex—" She wrapped her arms around
her middle, her voice breaking. "I only wished
you'd have told me the truth. Then I wouldn't
have to feel so embarrassed now, and you
wouldn't have had to endure all those silly, naive letters from a gushing coed."

"Is that what you . . . ?" He ran his hand
through his thick hair, groaning in new frustration. "That's *not* what I thought."

"It's okay," she said as she lifted her chin in
an attempt to regain her usual composure. "I
know I was very naive back then when it came
to relationships. I've known for years that you
didn't feel the same way about me that I felt
about you. It's just that I always thought . . .
I mean, I'd hoped that for a little while at least
you did genuinely care about—hey!"

He grabbed her arm and yanked her uncer-
emoniously away from the fireplace. "Hey,
what's the—"

"Quiet!" he commanded without turning
around. "All this blubbering is giving me a
headache."

"Well, I'm sorry, but that's no reason to
drag me around like some Neanderthal—" She
stopped talking, realizing he wasn't listening to
her. "At least tell me where we're going."

"Bedroom," he stated simply.

Suddenly embarrassment seemed the least

of her worries. "I don't think that's a good idea," she suggested cautiously.

He gave a short, harsh chuckle. "I don't care."

No, he didn't care. She'd poured out her heart to him, confessing that she'd once loved him. Apparently he was going to take advantage of that past feeling in the crudest possible way. *And to think I trusted him.*

He took the first stair. She grabbed the rail, jerking them both to a halt. "I think we need to talk about this."

"I'm through talking, Angel," he said, pulling her roughly against him. "It's time for deeds, not words."

His dark eyes glittered into hers, consuming her like dark fire. His warm, musky smell filled her senses, making her weak in the knees from something other than fear. Sexual awareness careened through her like a runaway bus. This is crazy, she thought as her eyes riveted on his full, sensuous mouth. I couldn't possibly want him to kiss me. Not now.

Whether she wanted him to or not, he didn't. Turning, he dragged her along like a recalcitrant dog on a leash until they reached the bedroom, where he let go of her with a suddenness that made her stagger. "Sit down," he ordered, pointing to the bed.

So much for foreplay, she thought. She rubbed her wrist, following his gaze to the bed.

She didn't think it was possible to feel more vulnerable about this unpredictable, explosive, sexually arousing man. She'd been wrong. In desperation, she tried reasoning with him.

"I just want to remind you that I saved your life yester—"

"Sit!"

She dropped to the bed without another word.

She went rigid, waiting like a sacrificial lamb for his next move. But instead of heading for the bed, he went to the rolltop desk. "I noticed earlier that you jimmied the lock. Nice work, but you missed one drawer."

"Is that why you dragged me up here? To discuss property damage?"

"Hardly." He switched on the small brass desk lamp and bent down to open the last drawer. "We're here for a history lesson."

History? The only history she had with him was short and painful, both in the past and in the present. She bit her lip, wishing there was a statute of limitations on stupidity. And on love.

She watched him search through the drawer. The faint gleam from the lamp threaded light through his shaggy, raked-through hair, giving his shadowed form a completely inappropriate halo. Like a fallen angel, she thought, with an equally inappropriate compassion. *I can't feel this way about him. It's tearing me apart.*

But whether she could or not, she did. She watched him from the shadows, drinking in his confident movements with a hungry fascination. Part of it was sexual—there was no denying that. But part of it was a need that came from a deeper part of her, a feeling so strong, it robbed her breath. She was bound to this man in ways she couldn't even begin to understand, ways that struck right through to her core.

For years she'd existed on the memory of their love. She'd endured life but she hadn't lived it, not until Curt blasted away all the icy loneliness in her soul. Dr. Osbourne had said that the reason she didn't get involved with another man was her lack of trust, but that wasn't true. The reason she didn't get involved was because she couldn't. Years ago she'd given her heart to one man, only one man. And with an awareness torn from the deepest part of her soul, she admitted he would hold her heart until the day she died. *Even though he never really cared for—*

"You wanted to know what it was like in South America," he said, interrupting her thoughts.

She pushed back her hair, looking at him skeptically. "You already told me. It was very difficult."

"Difficult?" he replied, his shadowed profile displaying a less-than-pleasant smile. "Learning to drive a stick shift is difficult. Buying a company at a bargain price is difficult. Working in the fields was pure and unadulterated hell.

"The place was a mud hole, full of filth, disease, and cruelty of the worst kind. Little kids died like flies of starvation, or were deformed from malnutrition. You can't imagine the poverty." He stroked back his hair, then fastened his dark gaze on her face. "I never *wanted* you to imagine it."

She shivered, feeling suddenly out of her depth. She'd lived in the street for a handful of months, but her experience was nothing like the complete, lifelong despair he was talking about. "If it was so awful, why didn't you—"

"Leave?" he finished with a grim laugh. "I had a little problem with money. And a bigger one with pride. The wells weren't much, but they were everything I had. Well, almost everything."

He pulled a thin packet of papers out of the drawer and held it like it was made of solid gold. Gingerly, he handed them to her. "They're a little worse for wear, but I figure you'll still recognize them."

"My letters," she whispered in wonder as she turned the dog-eared, mud-spattered, daisy-bordered papers over in her hands.

He settled his hip on the edge of the desk, watching her. "Those letters kept me going," he said in a low, almost reverent tone. "Sometimes I think they were the only thing that kept me sane. I used to read them at night so I could dream about what life had been like in Texas." He ran his hand over his face and added softly, "So I could dream about the girl I loved."

The girl I loved. She pressed the letters to her heart, feeling the icy wall she'd built around herself shatter into nothing. "You should have told me," she whispered, barely able to breathe from happiness. "I'd have come, no matter what it was like—"

"Why do you think I lied?" He got up from the desk and walked over to her, staring down at her from what seemed to be at once a few feet and a million miles. "I couldn't have watched you live like that. And if we'd had kids . . ." He shook his head. "I shouldn't have told you now, but I didn't want you to think that . . . In any case, it doesn't matter."

"How can you say that?" she cried, lifting her shining eyes to his.

In the light of the lamp he saw it all—the years of pain and emptiness, of a broken soul patched together by a veneer of elegant, icy reserve. Regret stabbed through him like a knife, but he knew he'd have regretted it more if he'd told her.

"It doesn't matter, because I'm not the same man I was back then. You don't know me anymore, not really," he said as he reached down and brushed away a tear she didn't even know she was crying. "And if you did, you sure as hell wouldn't want me."

He dropped his hand, forcing himself to back away from her. Touching her just made the good-byes more unbearable. "Promise me you'll go straight to the police after I leave."

She nodded and lowered her gaze to the ground, saying nothing. She hates me, he thought, feeling the cut much deeper than he expected. Well, maybe it's better this way. No tearful good-byes. No promises we can't keep. No regrets. *Like hell.*

"Where will you go?" she asked in a voice so soft, he almost missed it.

"It's better if you don't know that," he said, having a hard time keeping his voice level. She looked so damn vulnerable perched on the edge of his bed, like a baby bird that was about to fall out of a tree. He knew he had nothing to offer her but trouble. *Let some other white knight save her. My armor's rusted through.*

He dug his hand into his pocket and pulled out her keys, tossing them onto the bed beside her. Never look back. But he did look back, just once. He memorized the curve of her neck, the slope of her shoulders, the exact moonlight color of her spun-silk hair. He burned her image into his mind, to carry her with him through all the long, loveless years ahead. Then he turned on his boot heel and headed for the door.

"We're not going to see each other for a long time, maybe never, are we?"

"Considering half the cops in Texas are on my tail, I'd say that's a pretty safe bet."

She drew in a deep, steadying breath. "Then would you do one last thing for me before you go?"

"Sure," he said gruffly. "Name it."

Like a woman in slow motion she raised her tear-filled eyes. "Make love to me," she whispered.

TWELVE

Earlier in the day he'd suspected she was crazy. Now he was sure of it. He looked at the sane-appearing figure sitting on the bed with her pale hair tumbling over her shoulders, and tried not to think about how that silky fall would feel spread over his naked chest. *Christ, she's not the only one who's crazy.* "You can't be serious."

"Why not?" she replied, biting her lip in a way that made her look like a schoolgirl and a siren at once. "It's very nineties for a woman to ask a man to go to bed with her. Happens every day."

"Not when that man is a wanted criminal!"

"I don't see what that's got to do with it," she replied indignantly, rising from the bed. "After all, you aren't guilty."

Not of that crime, he thought, watching

her come toward him. She had the most wonderful way of moving, like a young colt that had just been released in a spring pasture. Sweet. A little wild. And provocative enough to tempt a saint. Even in that shapeless sweater and oversized skirt, the sway of her hips aroused every one of his very unsaintlike senses.

"Lyn," he said in a voice coarse enough to blister paint from a wall, "there is no way in hell I'm going to make love to you."

His harsh words worked. She came to a dead stop a few feet away, her confident smile crumbling. She tried to shove her hands into the pockets of her skirt, but couldn't seem to find them. Failing that, she put her hands behind her back, in a fidgeting movement that was at once graceless, awkward, and achingly endearing.

"I'm sorry," she said in a tone that strove for her trademark cool sophistication and failed miserably. "I thought that because you used to . . . but of course, tastes change. There's no reason to assume that because you found me attractive once, you'd still . . ."

She was breaking up inside. He could see it in the brave tilt of her chin and the forced, too bright smile quivering on her lips. So what's that to me? he thought, his jaw pulling ruthlessly taut. Let her think I don't want her. No one ever died of a broken heart. It's better this way. It's—

"Oh hell," he cursed as he reached out and yanked her roughly into his arms.

She toppled against his chest, but it was Curt who felt unbalanced. Ever since Saltsgaver's murder he'd been zooming along full speed on a roller-coaster car that was plunging straight down into oblivion. He didn't mind so much for himself; he'd been in dangerous, desperate situations before and come through with his hide intact. But this time he'd had a passenger in the car with him, an innocent, brave-hearted woman who was as out of her depth as a minnow in the middle of the sea. A sweet, conscience-numbingly sexy minnow who felt like heaven in his arms . . .

"You've got to get out of here," he groaned, pushing her roughly away. "Whatever we feel about each other, I'm still a wanted man."

"*Very* wanted," she agreed with a shaky, trembling smile.

"That's not . . ." He ran his hand over his face, feeling out of his depth himself. "If I made love to you now, I'd never forgive myself. I don't know when—or even if—I'll ever catch the bastard who killed Saltsgaver. I can't promise you a future."

"I'll wait," she said, stepping closer.

"That would be worse," he said, his voice

an open wound. "I've already gotten you far more wrapped up in this mess than you deserve to be. To think of you wasting one more moment of your precious life on me . . ."

He raised his eyes to the ceiling and let out a deep, ragged sigh. The wound in his side was beginning to ache again, but it was nothing compared with the pain in his heart. "Don't you get it, Angel? I love you too damn much to keep you with me a minute longer. I can't give you a future. Hell," he added with a harsh laugh, "I can't even give you tomorrow."

"Then give me tonight," she whispered huskily as she reached up and cradled his cheek against her palm. "Please, Curt. It might be all we ever have."

Her crystal eyes were a wide, shimmering window to her soul. In an instant he saw everything—the pain and loneliness, and the sweet, impossible love she still felt for him. There was no time to share that love. There was no time for anything else. He arched her neck and lowered his mouth to hers, moving across her lips with a profound tenderness. She'd been the most precious thing in his life, and he'd hurt her more than he could bear. *And God help me, I'm about to hurt her again.*

He cupped his hand around the back of her neck, pulling her instinctively into a sweeter, hotter caress. *Give me tonight*, she'd asked. Well, he could give her one night to make the pain in her lovely, loving eyes go away. Deep wounds needed fire to heal them—the fire of passion, of sex, of love. . . .

She buried her fingers in his hair as she slanted her mouth into a wilder, wetter kiss. Seven years of longing burst inside him, saturating his senses. He pushed her back into the soft covers of the bed, kissing her thoroughly, completely, madly. He bunched up her skirt and rubbed the hot silk of her thighs, taking her moans of pleasure into his mouth. Her hands were all over him, caressing him with a boldness that nearly took the top of his head off. Sexual hunger seared away any pretense of foreplay. He'd been starving for seven years; it was time to satisfy his hunger.

Her senses reeled. She forgot about Salty, the murder, the past, the future—everything except the man on top of her, his mouth hot and tasting of passion. With shaking hands she undid the buttons of his shirt, nearly frantic in her need to feel him against her, with her, in her. She yanked back the shirt and combed her fingers through the soft hair of his hard-packed chest. I did the same thing yesterday, she thought with a trembling smile. How could I have been so clinical?

She stroked her fingers down his side, loving the feel of his skin, like velvet over steel. Before she realized what she was doing, her hand touched the forgotten bandage, making him wince. Concern filtered through her passion-drugged mind. "Curt, your wound. Maybe we shouldn't—"

"God, don't even think it," he growled as he placed searing kisses against the side of her throat.

"But if you're hurting—"

"It'll hurt more not to," he said, his voice strained past the breaking point. He raised his head, his shaggy hair tousled like a lion's mane. He looked down at her with a gaze so raw with need and tenderness, it felt like a caress itself. "I need you, Angel," he confessed with rough, desperate desire. "I've needed you for seven long years."

Their mouths met in a primal hunger that ripped through them like a maelstrom. She was still shuddering from the ecstasy of the kiss when he pulled her sweater over her head, still quaking with its power when he stripped off her skirt and panties. I'm dreaming, she thought as she reveled in the delight of his mouth teasing her straining breast to an aching peak. But if it is a dream, I never want to wake up.

Reality and fantasy seared together. She felt the press of his knee against her legs, and parted them for him as she'd dreamed of doing in a hundred feverish dreams. Lost in dark, silent wanting, she felt his hand slide to the triangle between her legs, seeking and finding every hot, damp place, touching and caressing until she writhed against him. Her swollen flesh wept for his loving touch, but she wanted more. She needed more. There was an emptiness inside her, a hollow, aching loneliness that only he could fill.

He felt her trembling hands find his belt and unfasten it, then start to pull down the zipper. A shudder ripped through him as she brushed her gentle fingers against his straining erection. Memory and reality forged into one, burning out all the empty years of his life. And with that searing shudder, his stone heart turned to living, loving fire.

She opened herself to him, and the poignant sweetness of her well-remembered surrender sent desire raging through him like an oil fire. To hell with his gunshot wound, he thought as he positioned himself above her. He had another more important wound to heal—her broken heart. The veins in his arms stood out as he held himself above her, easing himself into her an inch at a time, fighting the overpowering need to bury himself in one thrust into her incredible, healing warmth.

His control began to slip when she arched her hips, and again when she slid her hands over his shoulders. But when she whispered his name he was lost. This wasn't a figment of his imagination; the girl he had loved was the woman in his arms. The beautiful blue eyes that had haunted his dreams shone up at him with love and trust so complete, it almost made him take his complete pleasure in her warm, tight body. But he wanted this moment to last until the past was forgotten, until the only thing that existed in their world was each other.

He moved inside her, slowly and steadily at first, then building to a driving force that left both their hearts thundering. He watched in silent triumph as love broke in shuddering waves across her face. He wrapped her in his arms and turned her, until their positions were reversed. The shock and delight on her face was past bearing. She bent down and placed an erotic, openmouthed kiss at the hollow at the base of his throat. "Please," she said huskily. "Please, love."

Love. For seven years he'd been waiting to hear that word on her lips. With a groan torn from the deepest part of him, he drove into her, plunging again and again until they were both wild with wanting. He couldn't give her a future, but he could give her a moment of forever. And in a final blinding thrust he took them both over the edge of white-hot oblivion, where all their past pain and heartache was destroyed in the burning, exploding, refining glory of their love.

"At least let me make the coffee," Lyn said glumly as she sat perched on the kitchen counter. "I want to help and you always said I made good coffee."

"I lied," he replied, measuring another scoop into the filter. "I only told you that because I wanted to get into your good graces . . . among other things."

She smiled, feeling the radiant warmth of their recent lovemaking curl through her. "You're uncouth."

He grinned, shooting her a glance so sizzlingly erotic, it turned her knees to water. "So are you, Angel. You just spent last night proving it."

"With a little help," she replied, shooting him a sizzling glance of her own.

They stood for a moment, sharing a smile that brought back every moment of the passionate night they'd spent locked in each other's arms. The memory sent a white-hot jolt of desire tearing through her usually conservatively cool body.

Not that she'd been particularly cool lately. Somewhere after midnight she'd changed his bandage, using several procedures that were probably not among the AMA-approved ministrations. Afterward they'd returned to Curt's bed and, despite her less-than-heartfelt protests, taxed his strength all over again. Near dawn they'd finally left his room, driven out by the only appetite they hadn't been able to satisfy in each other—the need for food.

"I'd still like to help," she said, scooting off the counter. She pulled closed the collar of his too large terry robe and pushed up the sleeves. "How about if I make toast? That's harmless."

Curt arched a warning brow, but pointed to the pantry. "There's some English muffins in there, I think. Benny gets someone to stock the pantry while I'm away."

"You're very fond of him, aren't you?" she said as she pulled the package of muffins from the shelf.

"He's like family. Actually, he's closer than family, since I almost never see my sister—except when she needs money."

"Yeah, well, I'm not exactly a member of the Cathy Brennermen fan club," Lyn confessed as she walked back to the kitchen. She opened the package and dropped a couple of the muffins in the toaster. "She burned down our barn and almost got my father killed."

Curt's smile turned sober. "Your family doesn't have much to thank the Brennermens for, do they?"

"Just one thing." She went up behind him and wrapped her arms tightly around his middle. "Just one very dear, important, essential, wonderful thing."

He turned in her arms, pulling her against him. He curved his palm to her throat and stroked her sensitive lips with the rough pad of his thumb. "What happened to uncouth?" he asked in a husky whisper.

"I'm getting to it," she replied in a voice just as breathless as his. His dark eyes stared intently down into hers, but they were no longer made of hard obsidian, but of warm, loving fire. The demons that had ridden his soul were gone, burned out by the consuming, healing inferno of their passion, and the bottomless depth of their love for one another. She burrowed into his warm, fur-dusted chest, drinking in the smell, the feel, the impossibly wonderful reality of his love for her. Nothing was going to keep them apart again.

Nothing, an inner voice reminded her, *except a murder charge*.

A chill crept into her heart. "Do you really think someone from Guardian killed Salty?"

"Your boss thought someone was dipping into the company till," he replied with a shrug as he turned back to the coffee. "That, combined with the bogus tape, makes them the most likely suspects. Me excluded, of course."

His tone was light and joking, but she wasn't fooled. Last night had bound them in body and soul, into one heart and mind. With a lover's instinct she heard the slight but undeniable uncertainty in his voice—an uncertainty that echoed through her. She knew he was innocent, but she also knew that the police still believed he'd killed Salty. He was still a wanted man. She pushed back her wildly tumbled hair, feeling helplessness close in around her. *Everything in the world has changed for us, and yet nothing has changed at all.*

She leaned back against the counter and twirled a strand of her pale hair around her finger. She was frightened for him—more frightened than she'd ever been in her life. But she was just as determined to put aside her fears to help him. *We've just found each other again. I won't lose him because some rotten bastard framed him for a murder he didn't commit.*

"There's only a couple of people who have the technical expertise to tamper with the array —besides me, of course."

He poured two mugfuls of coffee as the corner of his mouth edged up. "I think we can leave you out of the suspect list. Who are the others?"

"A couple of systems designers, Ric Bostick and Adeleous Thompson. But neither of them was at the gala."

"Okay, for the moment we'll put them at the bottom of the list. Who else?"

She took a bite of her toasted muffin, chewing thoughtfully. "Well, there's Jesse—Jesse Katz. He's the chief designer of the array matrix, so he definitely has the technical knowledge. But I just can't see him as a murderer. He's a little wild, and he had no love for Salty, but deep down I think he's nothing more than a scared, lonely kid."

Curt walked over and stood beside her, putting his arm around her shoulder. "Kids can pull triggers, too, Lyn."

"Yes, but he doesn't care about money. All he lives for is his computers. He can barely balance a checkbook, much less mastermind an embezzling scheme. Peter even has to remind him to cash his paycheck.

"Peter Shaw?" he said, his smile turning to a grimace. "Wasn't he the stuffed shirt who was all over you at the gala?"

She gazed up at him mischievously, loving his undisguised, endearing jealousy. "Peter's just a good friend."

"Why isn't he a suspect?"

"Peter!" she cried, laughing. "Don't be ridiculous. He could never murder anyone. He's too . . ."

"Wimpy?" Curt suggested innocently.

"Well-bred," Lyn corrected with a stern glance. "Anyway, even if one of them did tamper with the array, that doesn't explain the tape of you and Salty."

Curt took a deep drag of his coffee, his brow creased in dark concentration. "Maybe they were actors."

"Not unless those actors were your twins," she said quietly.

"Another Curt Brennermen? Lord, I hope

not," he replied, giving her shoulder a playful squeeze.

His tone was light. Nevertheless, she felt the tension in his arms and heard the underlying strain in his voice. She slipped her arm around his waist, hugging him fiercely. "Don't worry, love. We'll solve this thing together."

He took a stray lock of her unruly hair and tucked it gently behind her ear. "Not together, Angel," he reminded her softly. "Remember, you're going to the police."

She stiffened, looking up at him in alarm. "But I thought . . . I mean, after last night . . ."

"I wouldn't have given up last night for anything," he answered with a sad smile, reverently stroking her cheek. "But it's Sunday morning now, and in the cold light of day, I'm still a fugitive on the run. I've got to go on. Alone."

A terrible pain squeezed her heart. She'd agreed to the bargain last night, believing she could live with it. But she'd been wrong. She'd been changed by his love, made and remade with every burning kiss, every searing, cherishing caress. Yesterday she'd been alone. Now she was half of their whole, incomplete without him. And the thought of being apart from him again was more than she could bear. "Take me with you," she said, her voice trembling. "I promise I won't be much trouble."

He gazed down at her with a smile so bittersweet, it ached her heart. "Angel, trouble is your middle name."

"I'll be good. Extra good," she promised. She gripped the edges of his robe, not caring if she sounded desperate. She *was* desperate. "I'll do exactly as you say. All the time. I won't get in your way—"

"Worrying about you would get in my way." He breathed deeply, wrapping her in a crushing embrace. He buried his face in her neck, drinking in the soft sweet smell of her. "I'm in love with you. The thought of you being in any kind of danger tears me apart."

"Tears me apart too," she confessed, blinking back frustrated tears. She sniffed inelegantly and rubbed her cheeks on the sleeve of her terrycloth robe. Then she lifted her chin, putting on a brave show in spite of the despair in her eyes. "You're right. We had a deal. I'll be all right, I promise. Don't worry about—"

"Hell," he muttered. His mouth came down on hers—hard, insistent, aching, wanting. Seeing her courageous, tearful, hauntingly beautiful eyes broke something open inside him. He couldn't stand the thought of leaving her behind. He couldn't stand the thought of taking her with him. The gut confusion was ripping him apart. "I never wanted to hurt you," he whispered against the soft torture of her lips. "And I always hurt you."

"It doesn't matter," she cried softly, melting against him.

"Matters like hell," he breathed, taking her mouth again. Her sweetness made him ache more than any physical wound. For seven years he'd lived a lie, telling himself that loving her wasn't as much a part of him as his bones and blood. She was sweet and hot and his, dammit, *his*. Her love had made him whole, giving him back his belief in the decent, true, and honorable things of life. She'd given him back his soul, and the only way he could repay was to get out of her life as soon as—

She went rigid in his arms. Confused, he raised his head, worried that he'd somehow managed to hurt her all over again. But she wasn't looking at him. Her startled eyes were focused on something beyond his shoulder. He spun around—and slammed full tilt into Benny's broad, surprised, and clearly fascinated expression as he gaped at them through the kitchen pass-through.

"Guess I shoulda knocked," he muttered sheepishly.

THIRTEEN

"Don't worry, boss," Benny said as he shrugged off his heavy coat. "I called in a few markers and got some guys to set up a smoke screen for me. The cops probably haven't even figured out I've left the hotel."

"You still took a hell of a chance," Curt replied crossly as he and Lyn left the kitchen. "I didn't want you involved. Besides, you knew I'd get in touch with you as soon as I could."

"Yeah, but I thought you could use some help. 'Course, it doesn't look like you need any . . . now," he added as his gaze strayed to where Lyn stood with the oversized robe clutched to her chin and her cheeks burning with embarrassment. "You're the pretty lady from the party, aren't you?"

The word *pretty*, along with Benny's wide, sincere smile, helped bring back some of her equilibrium. She held out the hand that wasn't clutching her robe. "Lyn Tyrell."

"Yeah, I remember," he said, gripping her hand and giving it a hearty shake. His gaze returned to his boss. "Looks like she likes you better now."

"Yes," Curt agreed softly. "She does."

He gazed down at her, gifting her with a smile so cherishing, it made her fall in love with him all over again. She felt humbled by the fact that this strong, proud man should love her, and grateful they'd had the chance to share their love with such consuming sweetness the night before. But in the midst of her happiness, a shadow crept into her heart. *Will we ever have the chance again?*

They stood for several seconds locked in each other's loving gaze, until Benny coughed and loudly cleared his throat. "Er, sorry to break this up, boss, but we need to talk."

"So talk," Curt mumbled roughly, his gaze still fastened on Lyn.

"We should . . . we've got to . . . oh, for heaven's sake!" Benny cried, throwing up his hands. He reached into the pocket of his discarded coat and pulled out several sheets of folded newsprint, holding them in front of Curt's nose. "A source I know at the *Fort Worth Star Telegram* smuggled me these early proof copies of a couple pages. It'll be on the stands this morning. The reporter was so hot for an exclusive that he kept it from the radio, TV, even the cops. But once this news hits the streets . . ."

"What news?" Curt wondered aloud as he unfolded the sheets. "The only thing I see here is an article about a monster truck rally at the Tarrant County Convention Center."

"Other side," Benny explained.

Lyn leaned closer, watching as Curt turned the sheet over. She was immediately blasted by a gigantic headline reading BRENNERMEN AND BOMBSHELL SPOTTED IN WEST TEXAS GAS STATION. "Oh Lord," she cried softly as Curt let out a stiffer curse.

Benny nodded, his grim look echoing their sentiments. "You two have been made. The sooner you get out of this part of the state, the better."

Bombshell, Lyn thought with a wry smile as she peered at her reflection in the bedroom mirror. If that station attendant could only see me now. Dressed once again in the oversized sweater and skirt, with her hair in a riotous tumble around her blue eyes and rosy cheeks, she looked more like a windblown farm girl than a sultry femme fatale. But that wasn't the only change in her.

Gone was Guardian's reserved managing program designer. Gone was the poised, private woman who'd kept her emotions under such strict control. Lyn's bright eyes and flushed cheeks were an outward sign of the profound, fundamental change that had taken place within her. *If Dr. Osbourne could see me now,* she thought as she stroked a comb slowly through her unruly hair. *She wouldn't recognize me.*

"Lyn! Hurry up!" Curt yelled from downstairs.

"Coming!" she called back, an almost unbearable happiness welling in her heart. Logically she knew that she should feel frightened and desperate; the newspaper article had made her a fugitive along with Curt. But the truth was, she was immensely grateful for the mistaken assumption made by the gas-station attendant. Now Curt had no choice but to take her with him.

It wouldn't be an easy life. Until the real murderer was caught, they'd be criminals in the eyes of the people she cared about. She would have to give up everything to be with him: her successful career, her supportive friends and, most difficult of all, her beloved family. Just thinking about the pain this would cause her parents brought fresh tears to her eyes. But the only alternative was giving up Curt. And she couldn't do that, not after she'd found that he still loved her—

"Lyn!"

She gave her hair a final brush, then left the bedroom and crossed along the gallery to the stairs. Light flooded into the living room through the picture window, filling every corner of the room. She looked down and saw Curt and Benny standing near the bottom of the stairway, their heads bent in a conversation so intense, they didn't immediately notice her. Lyn stopped near the top of the stairs, taking an extra, clandestine moment to study the man she loved.

He'd changed into his work jeans and shirt, and had donned an old sheepskin jacket that she recognized from his Texas days. In his worn clothes, with his stroked-back hair and his booted foot propped casually on the bottom step, he looked so much like his younger self that it brought a lump to her throat.

For seven years she'd lived without him, tolerating life rather than living it. But last night his glorious, cherishing love had exploded her old life into a million useless pieces. Last night wasn't just an extension of their old passion; it was a whole new wonderful creation, burning away all the pain and loneliness they'd suffered during their years apart. She had to be with him. She was meant to be with him. *It doesn't matter how difficult the future is. For me there is no future without him.*

She started down the stairs, but froze as she overheard Benny's distressed words.

"I don't think she's gonna like it, boss."

"It doesn't matter," Curt answered, his mouth growing stern. "When I leave here I want you to take her to the nearest sheriff's office. The important thing is to keep her safe, and the only place she'll be safe is with the police."

"Yeah, but what about the article? That guy at the station says you were going at it pretty hot and—"

"I know what the article says," Curt interrupted, looking in disgust at the crumpled newsprint in his hand. "But the truth is that she was my hostage. The only reason she kissed me in that rest room is because I was holding a gun on her."

Benny scratched his chin in thought. "You weren't holding a gun on her in the kitchen a minute ago."

No, Curt thought grimly. I wasn't. But that was after I discovered that our love for each other was still true and strong, even after all these years. He closed his eyes, reliving for just a moment the passion they'd shared last night. No woman had ever responded to him so completely, had given herself to him with such innocent trust and such wild, sensual abandon. The thought of being apart from her for even one minute filled him with a bleak emptiness that made his earlier years without her seem like a cakewalk. But he couldn't sacrifice her future for his.

No matter what they felt for each other, he was still a man on the run, and she was still an innocent bystander. Nothing had changed since last night—except that it was ten times harder to give her up than before. *A hundred times*.

"Forget about what you saw in the kitchen, Benny," Curt stated in a voice as rough as gravel. "Forget about everything except how this started. I needed her car and her computer knowledge—so I kidnapped her. Tell the police you found her here abandoned. Tell them you found her trussed up like a chicken, if you have to."

"I *know* she's not gonna like that," Benny muttered. "She's got a temper. She'll probably truss *me* up like a chicken before it's over. She's not the kind of lady a guy messes with."

You're more right than you know, Curt thought, touching his bandaged side. But the wound wasn't the only mark she'd left on him. Her love had branded his soul with a sweetness and hope he'd forgotten existed. She'd given him back his faith in tomorrow and, more important, his faith in himself. Her safety was more precious to him than his freedom. More than his life.

"She's the most important thing in the world to me, Benny. I don't have time to explain it now, but I'd give up my life to keep her safe. I'm counting on you to make the police understand that she had nothing to do with any of this. Eventually she'll see this is for her own good."

"Don't bet on it," commented a quietly lethal voice from above him.

Hell. He glanced up, his eyes colliding with Lyn's unwavering, dangerously determined gaze. *Not the kind of woman a man messes with.* "How long have you been standing there?"

"Long enough to know you're planning to leave me behind," she replied as she started slowly down the stairway. "Long enough to know that you're asking poor Benny to lie to the police about us."

Dammit, why does even watching her walk down the stairs make me hot? "It's the only way, Lyn."

"Is it?" she asked softly.

She moved like a poem—a sensuous, erotic poem. She reached the bottom of the stairs, pausing on the step just above Curt, apparently unaware that her softly outlined breasts were level with his eyes. Jesus, he thought as he dragged his gaze away from the almost unbearable temptation of her body. "Angel, I can't take you with me. You've got to go to the police."

She shrugged. "All right," she said simply.

"All right?" echoed the two men in disbe-lief.

"Certainly," she replied, brushing past Curt with a suspiciously satisfied smile on her lips. "I'll be happy to let Benny take me to the police. I've got a lot to tell them."

Something's wrong, Curt thought. I know that smile, and it means trouble. Turning, he followed her over to the fireplace, his eyes nar-rowing suspiciously. "What exactly are you planning to tell them?"

"Oh, nothing much," she answered as she leaned against the stone wall, twirling a strand of hair around her finger. "Only that what the gas-station attendant said was true. We *were* going at it hot and heavy in the rest room—and not because you had a gun."

"You wouldn't. You . . ." He gripped her shoulders, and let out a thunderous curse. "You are not going to tell them that. It's not true!"

"Maybe not," she said, raising her chin in challenge. "But the attendant will back me up. They'll think I'm your—what's the word?"

"Moll?" Benny suggested helpfully.

"Don't encourage her!" Curt roared at his friend. He turned back to Lyn, his eyes shining fiercely, desperately. "Don't do this, Angel. This isn't a game."

"Neither am I," she said quietly. "I've never been more serious. Send me back to the police, and I'll tell them I went with you of my own free will."

Lord, she was impossible. He closed his eyes, fighting a sudden agony in his head and his heart. "Once and for all you are *not coming with me*. I refuse to ruin your life."

"By sending me away?" she cried, her control finally breaking. "You tried that six years ago, and look what happened. You only made us both miserable. Anyway, it doesn't matter what I *tell* the police. They'll see the truth for themselves."

Smiling shakily, she lifted her hand to cup his cheek tenderly. "Darling, look at me," she said, her voice dropping to a husky whisper. "Do you really think I could convince the police—even for a second—that I wasn't hopelessly in love with you?"

No, he thought, falling into the blue depths of her wide crystal eyes. Her love for him shone out like a beacon in the night, a blaze of absolute and unyielding truth in a dark and confusing world. Years ago they'd charted a course straight for each other's hearts. Last night they'd reached their destination, celebrating their homecoming with beauty and passion, binding themselves to each other in every way a man could bind himself to a woman. They were two minds who thought as one, two halves of the same beating heart. And she could no more hide the love she felt for him than . . . well, than he could hide his for her.

Sighing, he pulled her roughly into his arms. "Okay, Angel," he breathed against the soft silk of her hair. "It's you and me from now on."

"Good call," she mumbled, her trembling words muffled against his shirt. "For a while I was afraid I was going to have to get tough."

"Lady, they don't come any tougher," he replied with a low chuckle. He pulled her close, until he could feel her heart beating next to his own. *Two halves of the same heart.* He tilted up her chin, planning to drink another kiss from her stubborn, sweet, irresistibly enticing lips, when a loud cough brought him back to the present. He raised his head and met Benny's pleased but exasperated expression.

"Sorry, boss, but the cops . . ."

"Right, the cops," Curt agreed, reluctantly loosening his hold on the woman he loved. "We'd better go."

She nodded, smiling a thousand smiles all at once. Then she walked over to Benny's brutish form and placed a soft kiss on his cheek. "Thanks for your help."

"Wasn't nothing," he mumbled, his cheeks flaming with unfamiliar embarrassment. "I'm just glad you didn't have to get tough with him. I think he'd lose."

"I know I would," Curt agreed with a laugh. He was about to run a gauntlet of police and highway sheriffs, yet he felt more light-hearted than he had in years. *Because she'll be with me.* "You're right, Benny. This lady looks harmless, but she packs quite a punch. She even dreams about gladiators."

"Really?" Benny replied, wide-eyed, his admiration growing.

"I do not," Lyn argued primly as she marched back to Curt. "I have *never* dreamed about gladiators."

"Sorry, darling, but you do," he replied as he took her by the hand and started for the door. "I heard you mention them in your sleep the first night you were here."

"That's silly," she said, hurrying to match her smaller strides with his. "I simply don't dream about things like that. I—" Suddenly she came to a dead stop, her eyes widening in what looked like terror, her skin turning almost as pale as her hair. "Oh my God . . ."

"Lyn? Angel, what is it?"

"Gladiators," she breathed in a hush. "That's how he did it." She paused as she lifted her gaze to his, a new hope shining in her heaven-blue eyes. "Curt, I know how he did it. I know how he faked the tape!"

I can't believe it, Lyn thought as she sat heavily on the stool at the kitchen counter. It was staring me in the face the whole time. "It was Jesse. He showed me how he did it the night of the gala. Damn, I should have known. But I didn't believe he could be an embezzler, much less a murderer. . . ."

"Lyn, take it easy," Curt commanded, placing his arm around her shoulders to calm her. "What are you talking about?"

"The tape—the police tape of the murder. Jesse used his digital rendering of his gladiator program."

"Digital what?" Curt asked.

"Who's Jesse?" Benny questioned.

Lyn threw up her hands. "Listen for a minute, will you? I'm still trying to work it out in my mind." She placed her clutched fists to her temples, her head spinning.

"Jesse Katz is one of the head designers at Guardian—the man with the earring. The night of the gala he showed me a graphics program he'd worked up from one of those old gladiator movies. He'd analyzed the movements of the actors in one of the battle sequences into a digital 'spine.' Then he'd mapped the patterns of a couple of the Kimbell art pieces stored in the array's memory banks over the spines."

Benny scratched his chin. "Mapped? You mean like a road map?"

"In a way. Points on the image are mapped —or digitally attached—to matching points on the animated spine. When the program advances, the image points are tracked along with the moving spine, so it looks like the image is moving. Or, in this case, fighting to the death."

"Computers can do all that?" Benny asked.

"It's called graphic rendering," Lyn said, nodding. "The technology's been around for years, but it needed faster computers to make it work. Jesse told me he'd been working on the program for months. He had the spine completely set up. All he needed was an overlay image of Curt and Salty."

"Which is where this theory breaks down," Curt said grimly. "Thanks for trying, Angel, but it won't wash. You said Katz used images stored in the computer for his program—images of the cataloged art pieces. And let's face it—Saltsgaver and I don't exactly qualify as art objects."

"You did that night," she explained, feeling elated as the separate pieces clicked into place. "The computer matrix array is basically a sophisticated digital camera. It takes three-dimensional pictures of anything that comes within its viewing range—whether they're paintings, sculptures . . . or even people. Salty was inside the array several times that evening when he was explaining the computer system to various customers. You were inside it at least once—when you came into the back gallery to talk with me. Remember?"

"I remember," he said, softly stroking her cheek. "By God, Angel. I think you may have cracked this thing."

"You'll be cleared," she cried softly, gripping his hand. She gazed up at him, seeing the shadows of strain and desperation begin to disappear from his eyes, like darkness disappears with the morning light. Little by little hope was returning to his heart. *And to mine.*

"That's it, then," he stated, his voice ringing with new power. "We'll leave here and go straight to the police—"

"No!" she cried, rising from the stool to face him. "You can't do that, not yet. We'll need proof."

"We have proof. The program—"

"The program is still vaporware as far as the police are concerned. They'll need evidence. If we tell the authorities, Jesse may get wind of it—in fact he's bound to, considering how rabid the press is about reporting every minute detail of this case. It'll take him a nanosecond to delete the program from Guardian's mainframe computers."

"Hell of a lot easier to get rid of than a smoking gun," Curt commented, his grim expression returning. "So what do you suggest?

We march into Guradian's Dallas office and steal Katz's programs?"

"Not all of us," she replied quietly. "Just me."

For a moment she wasn't sure if he'd understood her. Then his eyes crinkled in humor, and he threw back his head in a loud, unexpected laugh. "I was right—you *are* crazy."

"But if it's the only way to clear you—"

"Then I'll stay guilty," he replied, taking her by the shoulders. "I appreciate the offer, Angel, but there is no way I'm going to let you go up against this murderer alone."

"I'll be careful," she promised.

"You'll be dead," he stated, his expression winter hard. "This isn't some computer game, Lyn; this is cold, calculated murder. I'm not going to let you anywhere near that kind of danger. We'll stick to our original plan. And when we get across the border, I'll contact some discreet private investigators I've used in the past. They can look into Katz's actitivities, and maybe even get ahold of his program—"

"That'll be too late," she cried. "I've got to get at Guardian's computer—now. Every minute that passes gives Jesse another minute to get rid of his program."

"And how do you know he hasn't deleted it already?" Curt asked softly.

He watched as her brave expression collapsed into a ruin of doubt. He stared into her azure eyes, feeling her disappointment cut him more keenly than his own. It hurt like hell to give up the chance of proving his innocence, but it was nothing compared with the agony he would feel if anything happened to her. "Don't worry," he said, gently chucking her under the chin. "You figured it out. That's more than we had a minute ago. We'll make this guy pay for what he did. That's a promise. But first we need to get out of here to a place where we can both be safe."

"Across the border," she said, repeating his earlier words.

"Right. Once we're safe, we'll figure out our next move." He lifted his head, looking over her shoulder toward Benny. "We'd all better give the cops a wide berth for the moment. Think you can get back to Dallas without them finding out?"

"No sweat," Benny replied with a shrug. "They think I'm still in my hotel room, drinking beer and watching dirty movies. They're not looking for me."

"Or me," Lyn mused, her expression turning suddenly thoughtful. "The article said you were with a blue-eyed blond—period. They don't know who I am yet."

"And with luck they won't know until we're safely across the border," he stated, giving her shoulders a reassuring squeeze before he released her. "Which reminds me—we'd better get moving."

He started to turn away, but felt the slight tug of her hand gripping his sleeve. "It's going to be a long trip," she said, her gaze straying to the downstairs bathroom. "I'd better . . . you know."

"Yeah," Curt said, amused by her delicacy. "Go ahead, Angel. I'll wait."

Once again he started to turn away—and once again he was restrained by her hold. She looked at him, her eyes shining with all the love and trust they'd shared last night, and more.

"I want you to know . . . that is, I want to tell you . . ." Her words dwindled out as she stood on her tiptoes and pressed a swift, tender kiss on the hard line of his jaw. Then she darted like a skittish colt into the bathroom.

"Cute, but a little crazy," Benny commented as he watched her disappear.

"Yeah, but a man could die happy trying to figure her out," Curt replied as he brushed the spot on his jaw where she'd kissed him. "Anyway, you'd better get out of here. The police aren't going to buy that hotel-room story of yours forever."

"I can handle a few cops," the big man stated, as if piqued that Curt could even suggest he couldn't. "But that Katz kid, he's a whole 'nother ball game. I saw him at the party; he was switching out the names on all the hors d'oeuvres. Figured him to be a troublesome punk, but not a murderer. He sure had me fooled."

That makes two of us, Curt agreed silently.

"But then, I'm not always so good at reading people," Benny continued with a shrug. "Take your lady, for instance. When she left the room she looked about as torn up as a woman can get—like she was leaving you forever or somethin'. But she was only going to the bathroom."

Like she was leaving you forever, Curt thought, his brow darkening with suspicion. She wouldn't. Not twice. He strode to the bathroom door and tried the knob. "Lyn?"

"Hey, you're not in that big of a hurry," Benny protested.

Ignoring him, Curt pounded his palm on the door. "Lyn! Answer me or I'll—"

He stopped as Benny grabbed his arm and yanked him back. "Cut it out. The lady deserves some priv—why are you wincing?"

"Because of my side wound," Curt bit out, propping his arm against the wall to steady him. "She shot me."

"She shot you!" Benny exclaimed, his eyes growing wide as saucers. He would have said more, but at that moment both men were stunned to silence by the grinding sound of a starting car engine.

Curt's oath could have blistered paint. He took a step toward the front door, but the pain of his still-sore side held him back. "Benny, stop her."

Benny lumbered over and pulled open the front door, but he was too late. Lyn's Jeep was already heading down the driveway, throwing a spray of gravel behind it. Curt reached the door just in time to see her red taillights disappear around the bend. *Dammit, Lyn, you're going to get yourself killed.*

"She's pulled the hoses on the other cars," Benny cried from the garage. "It'll take half an hour to fix them."

Half an hour. Not long enough to put him in danger of being caught by the police, but long enough to make sure he couldn't catch up with her. He shook his head wearily, and caught sight of the open bathroom window. Like a greenhorn, he'd fallen for the same trick, not once, but twice. *Only the second time she's heading into ten times more danger.*

He went into the garage where Benny was diligently reconnecting the hoses on his truck. "I'm not going to Mexico."

The big man nodded. "I figured we'd be heading to Dallas after her."

More than his freedom. More than his life.

"*I'm* going to Dallas, but you're not. Not yet anyway," Curt said as he bent to help Benny with the hoses. "This murderer's been a step ahead of me all the way. It's time to even the odds—no matter what it costs."

FOURTEEN

The place was silent as a tomb.

Lyn walked down the deserted hallway of the Guardian Systems offices, her shoes making no sound on the thick, forest-green carpet. Twice she turned around sharply, sensing that someone was behind her, watching her, stalking her. But all she saw was the long, oak-paneled hallway with its robust brass fixtures, its antique furnishings, and its gold-framed collection of nineteenth-century western art.

She recalled that Salty had picked out every one of the expensive pieces himself; it was one of the things Peter, as CFO, had objected to. But walking down the hallway now, she felt very glad Salty had bought the items, no matter how exorbitant the price. The extravagantly decorated hallway held his essence, his bombastic, larger-than-life spirit. But it wasn't large

enough to win out over a deceitful, foul murderer. *I'll get the man who did this to you, Salty.
And to Curt.*

Curt. During the drive to Dallas she'd managed not to think about him—for about ten
seconds. By now he was heading toward the
Mexican border, and safety. That, at least, was
a blessing, but it was a bittersweet one at best.
She knew his heart, and knew that he'd likely
spend the trip reconvincing himself that she
was better off without a fugitive like him. And
she knew, with chilling certainty, that if she
didn't find Jesse's computer files and prove
Curt's innocence, there was a good chance that
she'd never see him again. She had to clear
him, for his sake, and for hers.

She came to the end of the corridor and
entered the back offices of the company.
Though less impressively decorated, they were
still plush and spacious—and eerily quiet. It
was Sunday afternoon; there was no reason for
anyone to be here. Yet as she hurried down the
silent hallway to Jesse's office, she felt the hair
on the back of her neck begin to rise—a nightmare instinct left over from her days on the
street. She reached for the knob to Jesse's office door and paused, trying unsuccessfully to
ignore the feeling. Try as she might, she
couldn't shake the certainty that someone was
nearby, hiding behind one of the empty cubi-
cles, just out of sight, waiting for her—

"Lyn?"

She whipped around, coming face-to-face with a thin, sandy-haired man who was dressed in a suit and tie despite the fact that this was the weekend. "Peter," she cried, her relief so intense, it momentarily unbalanced her. "I thought you were Jesse. Thank God you're not."

"A fact I've often been thankful for," he replied with a patently smooth smile.

Always the kidder, she thought as her racing heart returned to normal. "What are you doing here?"

"The police asked me to come in and collect a few reports. Demanded it, actually," he commented, his smile turning sour. "I suppose they're too busy chasing after Brennermen. By the way, why are you here?"

She paused, wondering whether she should take him into her confidence. But there was no sense putting anyone else in danger of Jesse's retribution. "Extra work." She shrugged. "You know how it piles up."

"Then why are you going into Jesse's office?"

"What?"

"I asked," he repeated, his smile growing brittle, "why are you going into Jesse's office?"

She froze, feeling suddenly confused. And something about Peter, her humorous and harmless friend, made her extremely uncomfortable. "I suppose I made a mistake," she said, stepping away from the man and the door. "Upset about Salty, I guess."

"Yes, poor Salty," Peter said, sounding too pat. "But the truth is he was bleeding the company dry. Brennermen would have done the same if he'd gotten ahold of it."

"That's not true! Curt would have made Guardian stronger and more competitive."

"Curt," Peter repeated. "I thought it might be something like that." He reached out, touching her cheek, then her hair. "Blue eyes. Blond hair. Though I can't quite think of you as a bombshell in that atrocious getup."

His touch was cold, vaguely repellent. Dammit, she thought, shaking off the feeling, this is Peter, my friend. I was going to date him, for heaven's sake. "You're right. I am the woman in the article."

"So you stood me up to make it with a suspected murderer? Rather shallow of you, Lyn."

"It wasn't like that," she said, realizing her apparent rejection must have hurt him. "Curt and I knew each other before. And he didn't kill Salty. I know it's hard to believe, but Jesse did it. He killed Salty, then used a program to frame—"

A loud beep from Jesse's office caught her attention. "Peter, someone's in there!" She turned and grabbed the knob, thrusting the door open. A quick scan of the small room showed her it was as empty as the rest of the offices. But the light was on, and the newspaper with the article about Curt and herself was spread across the desk. More important, Jesse's PC was on, and was running the gladiator program she'd come here to find. As she watched, the screen images morphed into the deadly familiar patterns of Curt and Salty. She watched in horror as they broke apart into a million fragmented pieces and were replaced by the bold words FILE DELETED. "No . . ."

She looked again at the newspaper on the desk, catching something she hadn't seen before. Peter's coffee mug was set on the desk just beside the telltale article. Not Jesse's—*Peter's*. And the coffee in it was steaming hot, as if it had been there just a moment before. . . .

She spun around. "Oh my God. You purposely deleted Jesse's gladiator program. Which means you knew it was used to fake the police tape. Which means—"

She stared in shock and horror at the man standing in front of her. The mask fell from his expression, revealing a cold, sinister man whose indifferent, passionless smile held no trace of remorse. "I'm afraid so," he said as he pulled a small revolver from his suit coat. "I'm sorry you found out, my dear. I honestly was fond of you."

————————◆————————

"But how?" Lyn asked as he dragged her along the corridor toward the back of the building and the freight elevators. "You're the CFO. You don't know the technical workings of the array."

"You started out in finance and learned computers," he reminded her without bothering to turn around.

Dammit, he's right, she thought, cursing inwardly when she realized she should have considered him a suspect from the first. "But why kill Salty?"

"Money, naturally," he stated as he punched the elevator button. "The money I took from the company accounts was only seed money. I intend to make a nice profit selling Guardian's security technology to various interested parties. Emerging nations are just getting into computer crime. It's a boom industry."

"That's what the police think Curt's doing —you must have been the one who told them!"

"That was inspired of me," he said with a chuckle that made her skin crawl. "I gave them enough details of my own operation to make it sound plausible. That's the secret of a good lie. Make it as close to the truth as possible."

He was lecturing her on criminal techniques. She would have laughed if she hadn't been scared to the bone. This man had Peter's face, Peter's voice, even Peter's sense of humor, but his eyes shone with the dead, metallic sheen of a man without a conscience. She didn't doubt he could kill her. She thought he might even enjoy it. "You won't get away with this," she said, trying to keep panic out of her voice. "Too many people know."

"Like who?"

"Like . . . Jesse! Jesse knows. You erased the file you made from his computer program, but he's bound to spot the similarities between his orginal and the police tape."

"If he does, he'll keep quiet. Katz is an alias; he has a record as long as my arm for robbery and computer vandalism under his real name. He was responsible for introducing several major viruses into the Internet, including the legendary Armageddon strain. If he went to the police they'd inevitably turn up that record—a chance I doubt he's willing to take."

The elevator doors opened. Peter shoved her inside, slamming her against the wall with a force that drove the air from her lungs. She leaned against the side of the car nursing an aching arm, her head spinning, her fear rising. "But why kill Salty?"

"He was getting too close," he replied as he calmly hit the button for the building's sub-basement. "I've got most of the security information my buyers requested, but not all. And they won't pay for anything less than the whole package."

"It must be a great deal of money if you're willing to kill for it," she said quietly.

"It is," he assured her, fingering the gun. "Saltsgaver had the bad sense to sell the company just as I was completing my operation. Even that bumbling fool couldn't miss the discrepancy when he started to examine the books. He had to be disposed of."

Disposed of. Like an outdated report. Like an old computer. Like her. She closed her eyes in pain, realizing that's all she'd ever meant to him. He had never been her friend. "And what about Curt?"

"He was more of a threat than Salty. As new owner, he was bound to review the accounts eventually, and when he did . . . Well, they both had to be dealt with. I was truly beginning to worry, until last month when Katz bragged to me about the computer modeling program he'd developed. It was child's play to get him to explain it to me. I realized I could use the gala to get rid of Salty and the new owner at once. It really was a brilliant solution."

"Not entirely," she reminded him. "Curt got away."

For the first time she saw the gleam of genuine anger in his eyes. "That bastard. I set up an airtight frame, and he escapes. With your help."

This isn't only about money, she realized, her terror building as she watched his calmly malevolent expression. This is about revenge. He's angry at Curt for destroying his perfect scheme. And he's going to take it out on me.

The doors whooshed open. Peter grabbed her arm and dragged her out of the elevator and down the short, barren hallway that led to the parking garage. He reached the door and shoved it open, forcing her into the starkly lit, cement-block hallway that led to the subterranean parking garage. She thought about screaming, or trying to run, but she knew he'd shoot her before she got three steps.

There was no one to hear her, no one to save her. She was going to die, and the only thing she could think of was that she'd left Curt without telling him good-bye, without kissing him one last time—

Suddenly the weak ceiling bulb over her head exploded into darkness. Lyn heard a sound like a battle cry, then was torn out of Peter's hold and shoved to the hard cement ground so forcefully that it knocked the wind out of her. Bruised and gasping, she raised her head and peered down the shadowed gloom of the corridor in front of her. The hallway's only other hanging bulb was careening wildly, throwing bizarre, surreal shapes across the walls and narrow linoleum floor. In the kaleidoscopic light she could make out two formless shadows locked together at the dark end of the corridor. The swaying light threw a band of brightness across them, illuminating one figure's sun-gold hair—

"Curt," she breathed, feeling an overwhelming surge of joy, then fear, then horror as she saw Peter raise his glinting gun and strike the bright-haired shadow to the ground. "No!"

Ignoring her sorness, she pushed herself off the floor and ran to his side. "Curt," she cried softly, dropping to her knees beside him.

He groaned, pushing himself to a sitting position. "Angel," he growled, "get the hell out of here."

"Not a chance," she said, helping him to scoot back until he was sitting against the wall. "You're supposed to be in Mexico."

"Too many tourists," he muttered, then winced as his hand went to his side, and then his leg. "Damn, I think I twisted my ankle. I'm getting too old for this."

"No arguments here," she said as brushed back his hair and tenderly examined the cut on his forehead. "It's not bad. You'll live."

"I wouldn't promise that if I were you," commented a chilling voice.

She turned slowly, and looked up at the dark outline of the man standing over them. And the small, deadly outline of the revolver that was trained directly on Curt's heart. Oh

Lord, she realized, she'd forgotten. For a brief, wonderful moment she'd actually forgotten. "Peter, please, not him. The police won't listen to him. He's not a threat to you—"

She stopped as she felt Curt's strong, warm hand cover hers. "Don't worry, Angel. This sidewinder's not going to kill either of us," he growled as he raised his angry gaze to Peter. "You might as well give up now, Shaw. The police will be here any minute."

Shadows hid Peter's face, but Lyn could hear the threatening smile in his voice. "You can't honestly expect me to believe that you'd alert the police and then show up here yourself. You'd be sticking your head directly into the law's noose. Why would you do anything so foolish?"

"Because I love her," Curt replied, his deep voice rumbling through the narrow hallway. "And when this mess gets straightened out, I'm going to marry her."

Joy welled up like a spring inside her. She knew it was ridiculous to feel so happy considering the circumstances—that they were alone in a deserted hallway with a loaded gun pointed at their hearts. Truthfully she didn't believe that Curt had called the police any more than Peter did. But as she looked into Curt's loving eyes all the rest ceased to matter.

She'd never believed the stories about people's lives flashing before them when they die.

She'd been wrong. She saw her life in an instant—and saw that most of it had been every bit as gloomy and narrow as the hallway around her. She'd been afraid of life, hiding first behind her stories, and later behind her safe, emotionless wall. But Curt's love had opened up the dark, dusty attic of her soul and brought her into the sunlight. She laced her slim fingers through his sure, powerful ones, feeling his radiant love pour through her like fire, burning away even the memory of her past fears and unhappiness. *Dr. Osbourne was wrong—people can change who they are. But only if someone loves them enough to help them try—*

Her thoughts stopped abruptly as she heard Peter's gun being cocked. Apparently whatever happiness they had was going to be short-lived. She went into Curt's arms, nestling against his broad chest. "I'm not sorry. Not for anything," she confessed as his arms wrapped her protectively. "And just for the record, the answer is—"

The world exploded around her. Light, sirens, shouts, and running people flooded the narrow hallway, hurting her eyes and her ears. She blinked, wondering for a moment if she hadn't been shot, and if this wasn't some high-tech version of the afterlife. Then her eyes adjusted to the light, and she saw a broad, familiar, and extremely unangelic face hovering over her.

"Sorry I couldn't get here sooner, boss," Benny apologized. "I went to the local police station like you said, but they didn't believe me. Seems everyone and their brother was claiming they spotted you. It took me forever to convince them I was on the level, and longer to explain how you'd been set up by someone at Guardian. But once I got it across to them, they brought me straight here by 'copter and—"

"That's great, Benny," Curt interrupted, wincing. "But could you save it for now and see if you could rustle me up a paramedic? My foot feels like hell."

This evens the score, pal, Curt thought as he watched his huge friend lumber off through the sea of blue-suited policemen. He scanned the milling crowd, stiffening as his gaze picked out the thin shape of a handcuffed Peter Shaw being led through the door at the end of the hall.

"You're better at picking friends than I am," a soft voice beside him said.

He turned, gazing into the impossibly blue eyes of the woman he loved more than his life. He forgot the madness around them, forgot everything in the wonder of her eyes. He'd been a hunter all his life, but he'd never really known what he was looking for. Not until now, after he'd come so close to losing her forever. He raised his hand and gently circled her throat, feeling his own tighten with emotion.

"If that bastard had hurt you—"

"But he didn't," she breathed, joy breaking like dawn across her face. "We're alive, darling. And nothing is going to separate us again."

"Better not," he murmured, lowering his head to kiss her. "Now, are you going to marry me, or—"

All at once the searing beam of a spotlight was shone directly in his eyes. "Mr. Brennermen, we need you to answer some questions. . . ."

"Bad timing," Curt grumbled as he reluctantly let go of Lyn. He watched as an officer helped her to her feet and led her away to her own set of questioning. She walked through the midst of the turmoil with her usual queenly grace, drawing a soft smile of admiration from his lips.

"You'd better marry that woman," said a monotone voice beside him.

He turned, looking in surprise at the stiff, bespectacled policewoman standing above him. She reminded him more of Joe Friday than Cupid. Nevertheless, his smile widened. "Is that an order, officer."

"No, but it should be," answered the deadpan woman as she efficiently flipped open her notebook. "Now, if you don't mind, I'd like you to reconstruct the events of last Thursday night. . . ."

FIFTEEN

Benny split the blinds and peered out the window of the Park Memorial hospital room. "Uh-oh, a CNN truck just pulled up. That makes the three major networks, Fox, several local stations, and God knows how many newspapers. . . ."

"So much for secrecy," Curt grumbled as he leaned back against the too soft pillows of the hospital bed. "Damn, I should never have let the doctors talk me into staying the night for observation. I feel fine."

"Well, you're not," stated a soft but unyielding voice beside him. "You have a mild concussion, an abdominal wound, a sprained ankle, and several scrapes and bruises. If the doctors hadn't made you stay overnight, I would have."

Curt turned his head, his frown softening as

he glanced at the woman who sat perched on the edge of his bed near his feet. The old sweater she wore had once again slipped down to expose her shoulder, stirring fires in him that had no place in an antiseptic-smelling hospital room surrounded by an army of vampire reporters. But his fierce desire was outdistanced by his even fiercer concern. Though she tried to hide it, there were dark, haunted shadows under her once innocent eyes, and her slim shoulders were bowed under a new weight. He swore softly, cursing himself for focusing on his own pain and not hers. His wounds could be cured by time and nature, but hers . . .

"Benny, go out and check on the reporters, will you?"

"But there's nothing to—oh, *I* get it," the big man said as he glanced meaningfully between the man and woman on the bed. Smiling hugely, he left the room.

"Subtle he's not," Curt commented as he pushed his bruised body up to a sitting position.

Lyn made a soft sound of protest. "You shouldn't. The doctor said you weren't supposed to move—"

"Hang the doctor," he bit out, railing like a chained dog at his invalid status. "Anyway, it's not me I'm worried about now. It's you. How are you doing?"

"Oh, I'm fine. Only a few bruises—"

"That's not what I meant," he said, his voice dropping as he studied her with a gentle yet penetrating gaze. "How are you *really* doing?"

The words hit home. She swallowed and wrapped her arms tightly around her middle, looking young and lost and achingly vulnerable. "Not so good. I trusted Peter. I thought he cared about me, but that was just part of his plot. He was using me. I know it sounds weird, but . . . I feel like I've lost two friends instead of one. Does that make sense?"

"All the sense in the world," Curt assured her. He reached out, absorbing her small hand in his strong, anchoring grasp. "I've been sold out by people I thought were my friends. Damn, I wish none of this had ever happened."

"I don't," she said softly, lifting her eyes to his. "I don't wish that at all."

Neither do I, he thought as he pulled her roughly against his chest. She was his world, everything he'd ever wanted, and more. He rubbed his cheek against the pale silk of her hair and breathed in her sweet, intoxicating scent, silently thanking a God he'd almost given up believing in for her safety. Her love had brought summer back to the stark winter of his soul. Texas summer. "You know, we should probably get a few things straight."

Her cheek was pressed to his chest, and

through the thin hospital gown he felt her lips pull into a smile. "Such as?"

"Such as I don't want a weekend wife. I want you with me every day, every hour, every minute. It'll mean giving up your job at Guardian."

She raised her head, gazing at him with eyes so full of love, they robbed his breath. "I remember something Salty told me. He said that the career track wasn't right for me. He said I needed a man who would love me so strong and hard that there wasn't any room for anything else in our lives, except for a few"—a rich blush crept up her neck to her cheeks—"except for a couple of babies."

"Only a couple?" he asked huskily, lowering his mouth toward hers.

"Well, for starters . . ." she murmured as his lips covered hers. His kiss was cherishingly gentle, and so full of sweet promise it nearly shattered her heart. She melted against him, letting her silent kiss speak her love in ways her words never could. Gradually the kiss changed, deepening into a steamy, laughing tangle of hands, bodies, and hearts.

"Damn," he breathed raggedly as he lifted his head and smoothed back her wildly tousled hair. "Forget drugs. Who needs modern medicine when you're around?"

"That's nothing," she murmured as she curved her fingers around the back of his neck, her eyes smoky with desire. "If you liked that prescription, you should check out my bedside manner—"

She was interrupted by a sharp rap on the door. Curt looked up, silently cursing every doctor to the deepest pit of hell. "Go away. I'm doing fin—"

The door opened anyway, admitting not the doctor, but an extremely distressed Benny. "Sorry, boss, but I couldn't stop them. They'll be here in a minute."

Reporters, Curt thought darkly, consigning them to the same infernal pit as the doctors. He glanced at the beautifully disheveled woman in his arms, mentally wincing when he imagined the crude spin the media sharks would put on this sacred moment. "Stall them, Benny. Do whatever you have to, but keep them out for another sec—"

"Forget it, Brennermen!" boomed an angry voice beyond Benny. The door shoved open, but the two people who entered weren't reporters. The first was a green-eyed woman whose long chestnut hair was hastily clipped back with a silver-and-turquoise barrette. The other was a lean, tall cowboy with graying temples and an expression angry enough to turn a charging buffalo.

"Mom! Dad!" Lyn cried as she sat up and self-consciously straightened her sweater. "What are you doing here?"

"Thank heavens you're all right," Sarah Gallegher Tyrell said as she wrapped her adopted daughter in a warm hug. "Your brother Rafe saw the CNN footage of Peter's arrest and recognized you and Curt as you got into the ambulance. He called us at Corners and we drove straight—"

"That can wait," Luke Tyrell interrupted, his furious glare trained on Curt. "First I want some answers, Brennermen. Like why, after all these years, you slink back into my girl's life and drag her into a scandal the size of the Grand Canyon—"

"Dad, it wasn't like that," Lyn protested.

"The hell it wasn't," Luke replied thunderously. "You've got a lot to answer for, Brennermen. And I want to know what you're going to do about it."

Luke's anger had been known to turn the knees of the bravest men to water. Curt didn't even blink. "What I'm going to do, sir," he answered evenly, "is marry your daughter. If she'll have me."

"Marry her?" Luke said, his brow softening in surprise. He leaned back on his heels and rubbed his chin, glancing between the lovers. "Is that what you want, Lyn, darlin'?"

She nodded and turned back toward Curt, her eyes brimming with tears of happiness. She looked into his dark gaze, seeing in it not the tortured shadows of their pasts, but the shining promise of their future. Long ago they'd shared a Texas summer together. Now that summer would never end. "Yes, Mom and Dad," she said quietly, her heart so full, she could barely speak. "It's what I've always wanted."

"That makes two of us," he said, his reverent tone telling her that his dreams were being answered too. He opened his arms to her, but looked away as a tremendous whoop sounded from beside the door.

"I knew you two were gonna get married," Benny cried, sporting a grin as wide as the Rio Grande. "As soon as the boss gets out of here, we need to celebrate. And it just so happens I know this great bar. . . ."

THE EDITORS'
CORNER

When renowned psychic Fiona hosts a special radio call-in show promising to reveal the perfect woman for the man who won't commit, four listeners' lives are forever changed. So begins our AMERICAN BACHELORS romances next month! You'll be captivated by these red, white, and blue hunks who are exactly the kind of men your mother warned you about. Each one knows just the right moves to seduce, dazzle, and entice, and it will take the most bewitching of heroines to conquer our sexy heroes' resistant hearts. But with the help of destiny and passion, these die-hard AMERICAN BACHELORS won't be single much longer.

Riley Morse creates a sizzling tale of everlasting love in **KISS OF FIRE,** LOVESWEPT #766. He'd been warned—and tempted—by the mysterious promise that his fate was linked to a lady whose caress would strike sparks, but Dr. Dayton Westfield knows that playing with fire is his only hope! When Adrienne Bellew enters his lab, he feels the heat of her need in his blood—and answers it with insatiable hunger. Weaving the tantalizing mysteries of a woman's sensual power with the fierce passion of a man who'd give anything to believe in the impossible, Riley Morse presents this fabulous follow-up to her sensational Loveswept debut.

Victoria Leigh turns up the heat in this breathlessly sexy, faster-than-a-bullet story of love on the run, **NIGHT OF THE HAWK,** LOVESWEPT #767. She'd pointed a gun at his head, yet never fired the weapon—but Hawk believes the woman must have been hired to kill him! Angela Ferguson bravely insists she knows nothing, no matter how dark his threats, but even her innocence won't save her from the violence that shadows his haunted eyes. When a renegade with vengeance on his mind meets a feisty heroine who's more than his match, be prepared for anything—Victoria Leigh always packs a passionate punch.

THRILL OF THE CHASE, LOVESWEPT #768, showcases the playful, witty, and very sexy writing of Maris Soule. He's a heartbreaker, a hunk whose sex appeal is hard to ignore, but Peggi Barnett is tired of men who thrill to the chase, then never seem willing to catch what they've pursued! Cameron Slater is gorgeous, charming, and enjoys teasing the woman he's hired to redo his home. He'd always vowed that marriage wasn't on his agenda, but could she be the woman he'd been waiting for all his life? When a pretty designer finds that a handshake feels more like an embrace, Maris Soule sets a delicious game in motion.

Praised by *Romantic Times* as "a magnificent writer," Terry Lawrence presents **DRIVEN TO DISTRACTION**, LOVESWEPT #769. Cole Creek is almost too much man to spend a month with in the confines of a car, Evie Mercer admits, but sitting too close for comfort next to him will certainly make the miles fly! Sharing tight quarters with a woman he's fallen head-over-heels for isn't such a good idea, especially when a tender kiss explodes into pure, primal yearning. Terry Lawrence knows just how to entangle smart, sexy women with an appetite for all life offers with the kind of men the best dreams are made of.

Happy reading!

With warmest wishes,

Beth de Guzman

Shauna Summers

Beth de Guzman   Shauna Summers

Senior Editor   Associate Editor

P.S. Watch for these fascinating Bantam women's fiction titles coming in December: With her spellbinding imagination and seductive voice, Kay Hooper is the only author worthy of being called today's successor to Victoria Holt; now, she has created a unique and stunning tale of contemporary suspense that begins with a mysterious homecoming and ends in a shattering explosion of passion, greed, and murder— and all because a stranger says her name is **AMANDA.** *New York Times* bestselling author Sandra Brown's **HEAVEN'S PRICE** will be available in paperback, and Katherine O'Neal, winner of the *Romantic Times* Award for Best Sensual Historical Romance, unveils **MASTER OF PARADISE**—a tantalizing tale of a notorious pirate, a rebellious beauty, and a dangerously erotic duel of hearts. Finally, in the bestselling tradition of Arnette Lamb and Pamela Morsi, **TEXAS OUTLAW** is a triumph of captivating romance and adventure from spectacular newcomer Adrienne deWolfe. Be sure to catch next month's LOVESWEPTs for a preview of these wonderful novels. And immediately following this page, catch a glimpse of the outstanding Bantam women's fiction titles on sale *now*!

Don't miss these extraordinary books
by your favorite Bantam authors

On sale in October:

BRAZEN
by Susan Johnson

THE REDHEAD
AND
THE PREACHER
by Sandra Chastain

THE QUEST
by Juliana Garnett

BRAZEN
by bestselling author
Susan Johnson

Countess Angela de Grae seemed to have everything a woman could want: wealth, position, and an exquisite beauty that had once bewitched even the Prince of Wales. But from the moment the dashing American playboy and adventurer Kit Braddock laid eyes on the legendary Countess Angel, he knew she was unlike the other rich, jaded blue bloods he'd ever met. For beneath the polish and glitter of her privileged life, he glimpsed a courageous woman tormented by a secret heartache. Determined to uncover the real Angela de Grae, what Kit found was a passionate soul mate trapped in a dangerous situation by a desperate man. And in one moment of reckless, stolen pleasure, Kit would pledge his very life to rescue her and give her the one thing she'd forbidden herself: the ecstasy of true love.

"How can we leave? Bertie's still here," Angela replied with a small sigh. No one could precede a royal guest.

Kit's eyes shone with mischief. "I *could* lower you over the balustrade and we could *both* escape."

Her mouth quirked faintly in a tentative smile. "How tempting. Are the festivities wearing thin for you too, Mr. Braddock? We were supposed to formally meet tonight," she graciously added. "I'm Angela de Grae, a good friend of Priscilla's mother."

"I thought so," he neutrally replied. He silently commended her for the subtle insinuation of the name of the young woman he'd been seeing lately, and thought her gracious for not flaunting her celebrity. She was a professional beauty; her photos sold in enormous numbers in England. "And yes, worn thin is a very polite expression for my current mood. I'm racing early tomorrow and I'd rather sleep tonight than watch everyone become increasingly drunk."

"Champagne *is* flowing in torrents, but Bertie is pleased with his victory. Especially after losing to his nephew last year."

"Willie deserved his trouncing today. He should have been disqualified for almost shearing off our bow on the turn. But at the moment I'm only concerned with escaping from the party. If I'm going to have my crew in shape in the morning, we're all going to need some rest."

"Do they wait for your return?" The countess's voice held the smallest hint of huskiness, an unconsciously flirtatious voice.

"Priscilla doesn't know, of course." Kit Braddock referred to his female companions as crew; reportedly he kept a small harem on board his yacht to entertain him on his journeys around the world.

"She's too young to know," he casually replied, "and rumor probably exaggerates."

The countess took note of the equivocal adverb but she too understood the demands of politesse and said, "Yes, I'm sure," to both portions of his statement. It was very much a man's world in which she lived, and while her enormous personal wealth had always allowed her a greater measure of freedom than that allowed other women, even Angela de Grae had at times to recognize the stark reality of the double standard.

"Well then?" His deep voice held a teasing query.

"I'm not sure my mopish brooding is worth a broken leg," Angela pleasantly retorted, rising from her chair and moving the small distance to the balustrade. Gazing over the climbing roses, she swiftly contemplated the drop to the ground. "Are you very strong? I certainly hope so," she quickly added, hoisting herself up on the balustrade and smoothly swinging her legs and lacy skirts over the side. "Although, Mr. Braddock," she went on in a delectable drawl, smiling at him from over her bare shoulder, "you certainly *look* like you have the strength to rescue us from this tedious evening."

How old *was* she? he found himself suddenly wondering. She looked like a young girl perched on the terrace rail, her hands braced to balance herself. In the next quicksilver instant he decided it didn't matter. And in a flashing moment more he was responding to the smile that had charmed a legion of men since young "Angel" Lawton had first smiled up at her grandpapa from the cradle and Viscount Lawton decided to overlook his scapegrace son in his will and leave his fortune to his beautiful granddaughter.

"Wait," Kit said, apropos her pose and other more disturbing sensations engendered by the countess's tempting smile. Leaping down onto the grass bordering the flower beds, he gingerly stepped between the tall stands of lilies, stopped directly below her, lifted his arms, smiled, and said, "Now."

Without hesitation she jumped in a flurry of petticoats and handmade lace and fell into his arms.

THE REDHEAD AND THE PREACHER

by award-winning author

Sandra Chastain

"This delightful author has a tremendous talent that places her on a pinnacle reserved for special romance writers."
—*Affaire de Coeur*

McKenzie Kathryn Calhoun didn't mean to rob the bank in Promise, Kansas. But when she accidentally did, she didn't think, she ran. Suddenly the raggedy tomboy the town rejected had the money to make a life for herself . . . if she didn't get caught. But it was just her luck to find herself sitting across the stagecoach from a dangerously handsome, gun-toting preacher who seemed to see through her bravado to the desperate woman beneath.

Assuming the identity of the minister had seemed a ready-made cover for his mission. Now, in the coach, he amused himself by listening, feeling, allowing his mind's eye to discover the identity of his traveling companion.

Female, he confirmed. The driver had called her ma'am.

A good build and firm step, because the carriage

had tilted as she stepped inside, and she'd settled herself without a lot of swishing around.

Probably no-nonsense, for he could see the tips of her boots beneath the brim of his hat. The boots were worn, though the clothing looked new. The only scent in the air was that of the dye in the cloth.

Practical, for she'd planted both feet firmly on the floor of the coach and hadn't moved them; no fidgeting or fussing with herself.

Deciding that she seemed safe enough, he flicked the brim of his hat back and took a look at her.

Wrong, on all four counts. Dead wrong. She was sitting quietly, yes, but that stillness was born of sheer determination—no, more like desperation. She was looking down at rough, red hands and holding on to her portmanteau as if she dared anybody to touch it. Her eyes weren't closed, but they might as well have been.

The stage moved away in a lumbering motion as it picked up speed.

The woman didn't move.

Finally, after an hour of steady galloping by the horses pulling the stagecoach, she let out a deep breath and appeared to relax.

"Looks like you got away," he said.

"What?" She raised a veil of sooty lashes to reveal huge eyes as green as the moss along the banks of the Mississippi River where he'd played as a child. Something about her was all wrong. The set of her lips was meant to challenge. But beneath that bravado he sensed an appealing uncertainty that softened the lines in her forehead.

"Back there you looked as if you were running away from home and were afraid you wouldn't escape," he said.

"I was," she said.

"Pretty risky, a woman alone. No traveling companion, no family?"

"Don't have any, buried my—the last—companion back in Promise."

Macky risked taking a look at the man across from her. He was big, six feet of black, beginning with his boots and ending with the patch over his eye and a hat that cast a shadow over a face etched by a two-day growth of beard. There was an impression of quiet danger in the casual way he seemed to look straight through her as if he knew that she was an impostor and was waiting for her to confess.

Across the carriage, Bran was aware of the girl's scrutiny. He felt himself giving her a reluctant grin. She was a feisty one, his peculiar-looking companion with wisps of hot red hair trying to escape her odd little hat. She had a strong face and a wide mouth. But what held him were green eyes that, no matter how frosty she tried to make them, still shimmered with sparks of silver lightning.

"I'm called Bran," he said slowly.

Bran decided she was definitely running away from something, but he couldn't figure what. He should back off. Planning the job waiting for him in Heaven was what he ought to be doing.

Bran had always found women ready to make a casual relationship with him more personal. They seemed attracted to danger. But this one didn't. And that cool independence had become a challenge.

Maybe a little conversation would shake the uneasy feeling that he was experiencing.

"What are you called?" he asked.

"Trouble mostly," she said with a sigh that told him more than she'd intended.

"That's an odd name for a woman."

"That's as good as you're going to get," she added, lifting a corner of the shade covering the open window.

Good? There it was again. "Good is a rare quality in my life." He took a long look at her. "But I'm willing to reserve judgment."

He was doing it again—extending the conversation. Something about this young woman was intriguing. "Truth is, I'm a lot more likely to appreciate a woman who's bad. Wake me when we get to the way station."

THE QUEST
by dazzling new talent
Juliana Garnett

"An opulent and sensuous tale of unbridled passions. I couldn't stop reading."
—Bertrice Small, author of *The Love Slave*

All his life, the notorious Rolf of Dragonwyck, known as the Dragon, has taken what he wanted by the strength of his sword and the fierceness of his spirit. But now his enemies have found the chink in his armor: his beloved son. With the boy held prisoner by the ruthless Earl of Seabrook, the Dragon will do anything to get him back. Yet when he decides to trade a hostage for a hostage and takes the beautiful Lady Annice d'Arcy captive, the seasoned knight is in for a shock: far from the biddable maiden he expects, he finds himself saddled with a recklessly defiant lady who has a rather dangerous effect on his body and his soul. Suddenly, the fearless Dragon wonders if he might win back his child . . . only to lose his warrior's heart.

Uneasy at his seeming indifference to her presence, Annice made no protest or comment when Vachel brought her a stool and seated her between Sir Guy and le Draca. The high table was at a right angle to the other tables lining two sides of the hall, giving an excellent vantage point. A fire burned in the middle. Supper was usually a light meal, coming as it did after evensong and sunset. It was still the Lenten season so platters of meat were replaced by broiled fish and trenchers of fish stew. Cheeses and white bread made up for the lack of meat. There was no lack of spiced wine, with cups readily refilled. Intricate subtleties were brought out for the admiration and inspection of the delighted guests. One subtlety was constructed of towering pastry and glazed honey in the shape of a castle complete with jellied moat.

'Twas obvious that the lord of Dragonwyck was not close or mean with his food, as if he did not suspect a siege might soon be laid at his walls. Any other lord might be frugal at such a time, fearing long abstinence from ready supplies.

Even the beggars common in every hall were being doled out fresh foods along with scraps; Annice saw servants burdened with huge baskets leave the hall. Frowning, she toyed with her spoon instead of eating. Was this show of abundance supposed to impress her with his indifference? Or had he already received an answer to his proposal, and knew he would not have to wage war?

Looking up hopefully, Annice noted le Draca's gaze resting on her. Thick lashes shadowed his eyes, hiding any possible clue, though a faint smile tugged at the corners of his mouth. He was too serene, too confident. He must know something. A courier could well have traveled to Seabrook and come back with a reply in a fortnight.

Her heart gave an erratic thump. P'r'aps she was about to be released. . . . Had negotiations been completed to that end?

She had her answer in the next moment, when he

leaned close to her to say, "I trust you will enjoy your stay with us, milady, for it seems that it will be an extended one."

The breath caught in her throat. One hand rose as of its own accord, fingers going to her mouth to still any impulsive reply. She stared at him. His lashes lifted, and she saw in the banked green fires of his eyes that he was furious. Dismay choked her, and she was barely aware of the intent, curious gazes fixed on them as she half rose from her stool.

Catching her arm, he pulled her back down none too gently. "Nay, do not think to flee. You are well and truly snared, little fox. It seems that your overlord prefers the hostage he has for the one I have. Or so he claims. Will he be so self-satisfied with his decision in the future, I wonder? Though I will not harm you, for concern that he might think it politic to do harm to my son, there are varying degrees of subjugation."

His hand stroked up her arm, brushing the green velvet of her gown in a slow, languorous caress that made her stiffen. One of her long strands of hair had fallen over her shoulder to drape her breast, and the backs of his fingers rubbed against her as he lifted the heavy rope of hair in his palm. He did not move his hand, but allowed it to remain pressed against her breast as he twisted the strands of hair entwined with ribbons between his thumb and fingers. Staring at her with a thoughtful expression, he slowly began to wind the bound hair around his hand to bring her even closer to him.

Annice wanted to resist, but knew that 'twas useless, even in front of the assemblage. None would stay their overlord. Helpless, she found herself almost in his lap, her face mere inches from his and her hands braced against his chest.

"It seems," Rolf murmured softly, his words obviously intended for her ears alone, "that your overlord regards me in the role of abductor rather than captor. Though there may seem to be little difference 'tween the two, there is a significant one. As abductor of a widowed female, I will be required to pay penance as well as a fine for taking you." An unpleasant smile slanted his mouth and curdled her blood. "Unless, of course, I receive permission from your next of kin—in this case, your brother."

"My . . . my brother?" Annice struggled for words. "But I have not corresponded with Aubert in years. We barely know one another, and—permission for what?"

Still holding her hair so that her face was unnervingly close, he grasped her chin in his other hand, fingers cradling her in a loose grip. P'r'aps she should have been better prepared. After all, it was not unheard of, though times had passed when it was common.

Still, Annice was totally taken aback when le Draca said in a rolling growl, "Permission to wed you, milady."